Comments on the approach to life described within these pages...

I will never be able to view health, disease and the process of healing solely through the lens of Western medicine again. The experience forever changed my approach to the practice of medicine. I recommend the experience to all without qualification.

Mark Warner, MD, Cardiologist

Learning Energy Medicine has deeply changed my life. Dorothy Martin-Neville's work provided me with the structure, guidance and emotional support for self-growth making me at peace with who I am and able to love myself as I love others.

Faith Parsons, MA, Licensed Professional Counselor

This work has brought me back to the TRUE reality of who I am and what my soul purpose is.

Lynn Rosario

This work has helped me to waken to the truth of who I am, to honor each and every step of my journey, and to discover the power I have to make my life everything I want it to be.

JoAnn Lopes

Comments on Your Soul Sings, Your Body Dances

Understanding the body/mind/spirit connection to wellness transformed not only my personal life, but also my artistic expression. Your Soul Sings, Your Body Dances is a must read for anyone wishing to live a healthy, joy-filled, purpose driven life.

Bonnie MacKenzie, Artis

Your Soul Sings Your Body Dances

Listening to Their Conversation

Dorothy A. Martin-Neville, PhD, DCEP, EMP

ISBN: 1450575722
ISBN-13: 9781450575720

This book is the result of over 20 years of working in the field of health care, serving those who came to see me while we each walked our journeys together. Learning to love, learning to see the real people who came into my office or my school, not their symptoms or their diagnosis, has permitted me to walk a journey of joy, adventure, awe, shock, wonder, and compassion, always learning from whoever blesses my life by walking in.

My children, Amy and Mike, who taught me to love in ways I never knew possible, and my grandchildren, Madison, Kaitlyn, and Colin, who bring such innocence and purity to my life, are the basis for so much joy and understanding of the unlimited qualities of human nature.

To all my friends, students, and clients who have taught me, laughed with me, and grown with me as we have walked together sharing our journeys, as we continue to learn and to grow, I thank you. You have made it so clear that we can never truly walk this path alone and still be whole. There is a richness within each of us that is beyond words; when we share it with each other it brings a fullness that completes me.

As embodied souls, as pure essence in human form, we are on a journey that is always beginning anew and yet continuing from where it was. I thank each of you for the challenge, the mirror, and the love. May we all celebrate the glory of the walk, in tears of laughter and joy.

Table of Contents

PART TWO

INTRODUCTION

Many of you were raised with the illusion that the body and the soul were in competition with one another. You were taught that they were fighting against each other with the winner defining whether you would end up in heaven or suffering the consequences of hell for all eternity.

There is another entirely new perspective available to you having nothing to do with that inner battle—one that instead allows you to see this journey as your opportunity to experience the depth of the intimacy that can exist between your body and soul. These two are not in battle at all but are actually attempting to be heard by your conscious mind so that the acknowledgement of this existing relationship can open you up to a completely new way of looking at your life, your health, and you.

After 25 years as a psychotherapist and Energy Medicine practitioner, I have come to believe without a doubt that we are embodied souls innately possessing a deep and profound connection between the spiritual and physical worlds to such an extent that our mental and physical health is often dependent upon our ability to listen to the conversation between our body and soul. We all innately possess a great soul-wisdom; learning to hear it and to listen to what it is saying can shape our entire life with ease, joy, inner peace, and always passion. Our soul, our mind, our emotions, and our body are programmed to work as one. We can feel it in our body when it is working, when we are "in the flow."

This is not my thinking alone since scientists such as Candace Pert and Brian Goodwin, as well as humanists such as Blair Justice and Deepak Chopra, discuss the relationship of expectations and beliefs, whether conscious or unconscious, to our physical health. Also, it has been several years since popular writers such as Barbara Brennan, Louise Hay, and Deb Shapiro began the process of bringing the impact of our spirituality on our health into public focus through their widely successful books, *Hands of Light*, *You Can Heal Your Life*, and *Your Body Speaks Your Mind*.

Even further, authors such as Larry Dossey, MD, and others in the medical community, have written of the power of prayer and spirituality in healing. With the convergence of all these publications reflecting the movement toward integration of the body *and* soul in medicine, wholistic health itself is, from my perspective, finally becoming officially whole by embracing an intrinsic aspect of who we are, our soul.

Have you noticed that when you are consciously listening to the body/soul conversation, you know when something isn't right? You know instinctively when something or someplace doesn't feel good or when something is off balance, even when you can't put your finger on just what that something is. At least you are listening and that can lead you to a whole new level of being alive.

Learning to pay attention to that knowing cannot only improve your level of awareness of the world around you but can also support you in being much more aware of your physical body, your physical health, and, most importantly, your soul's way of communicating with you. Learning to listen to that communication makes you freer, more alive, more passionate, and more real—put simply, more you.

My goal in writing this book is to support you in claiming all this and more. This book will help you understand how to hear and, how to listen to, your soul's messages as they are shared through your body. You can hear them, and feel them, and know what the messages are saying through your energy field and through your body awareness. When you choose to listen, and learn the language, the message is as clear as those you hear on your cell phone and yet so much more real, exciting, freeing, and physical. They are all about you.

Your Heart's Energy

Gary Swartz and Linda Russek write in the foreword of Paul Pearsall's *The Heart's Code* that the heart is the largest source of bioenergy in the body and that this energy travels through your skin into outer space. Pearsall credits Swartz and Russek with the development of the field of "cardio-energetics." For those who are unaware, this is a specialty that focuses on cellular memory and heart energy. I will address it further shortly.

Haven't you literally physically felt the love of another? Isn't it easy to bring that memory and that full-bodied experience to life, if you choose, through memory? Haven't you felt, physically, throughout your body, the love you have for another, whether a child, a lover, or a parent? Haven't you felt it pulsating through you? At those moments, doesn't it feel as if your soul is being touched, that the very essence of you is being experienced? That the core of who you are has been reached and caressed? In contrast, could a closed or defended heart be the result of losing connection to your soul's knowing and the intrinsic compassion your heart contains?

Your Body's Energy

The energy generated in your heart flows throughout your body combining with all the energy generated through physical movement or organic function. Your health on all levels, emotionally, spiritually, and physically, comes about when all that energy is permitted to flow freely and naturally. When it isn't, recognizing what is causing that energy to be stuck, stagnant, or deficient may be the secret to living healthy while also helping you in learning to live this journey passionately, vibrantly, and as alive as we are all meant to. Recognizing where it is stuck or deficient, when it is, and why, allows you to deal with the source of the problem and to understand how you deal with pain, pressure, or fear. We each hold those issues differently in our body; knowing how you do it gives you a far deeper level of self-awareness and an option to change to healthy patterns of dealing with them.

Rather than finding this perspective to be an entirely new concept, or even something unfamiliar, it may only be a step beyond your current thinking. Have you ever felt as if your heart was literally breaking during a period of extreme sadness? Was it telling you something at the time? Did your heart and soul know you would survive even if you felt as if you were dying? In regard to your body's experience, you have already experienced your energy field countless times, and yet may never have identified it as such.

You already know how the energy in your body is supposed to feel, without even realizing that you do. For example, when you know your health is not right, and yet, when you go to the doctor, s/he cannot find anything wrong. This is an example of your own inner knowing, your own awareness of your body on an energetic level. On a deeper level than you are usually conscious of, you sense an imbalance in your body, yet it cannot be detected through traditional medical tests. That is because all disease and disorders begin on an energetic level and only later appear on the physical plane. Disease begins energetically, moves to the spiritual level, then the emotional, and only later, if not resolved, manifests as a physical disease or disorder.

One of the important aspects of sitting in the quiet or in meditation is that while this sense of imbalance is still solely on an energetic level, you can become aware of it and can deal with it then, before it becomes a physical difficulty. The EEG and EKG are medical approaches to detecting energy imbalances early in only two areas of your body, yet in silence the imbalances can be detected anywhere in your body by you or by a well-trained practitioner who can feel the energy flow within your body with his or her hands.

Energy Medicine

Professional Energy Medicine practitioners have worked on this level for thousands of years in other parts of the world. They are aware of the many levels of health (emotionally, spiritually, and physically) and disease in the body and work with each one separately and yet as part of one holographic unit. As a result, if needed, while you are learning to listen again to what you may have lost touch with, Energy Medicine practitioners may support you in understanding what is being said. On your own, meditation, yoga, and reflection are all tools for listening, as well. Learning to sit in silence so the real conversation can begin is hard in a culture where being busy with unrealistic demands on your time is the norm. The rewards are worth the effort and time, nevertheless.

In supporting you, some practitioners have trained in one, two, three, or more approaches to the energy field. No matter what the extent of their training is, each body is still a mystery.

Each body has its own rhythm, its own dance. For a practitioner, this is what makes the work so enjoyable. Even though I have worked for over 20 years in this field, it still never ceases to amaze me and thrill me that I have been so blessed to be in this field. It has taught me about intimacy with another and a quality of silence that is mystical—experiences I never knew were possible.

There are numerous books on the market that treat these various approaches in great detail. Carolyn Myss has a wonderful book entitled *Anatomy of the Spirit* that describes some of this work. Anodea Judith has a comprehensive book entitled *Eastern Body/Western Mind* that discusses the blending of many of the areas of your energy field and how they are all connected.

How Your Energy Works

Every thought and every feeling you have ever had is an energetic reality. When you do not accept these thoughts and feelings, when you decide that you are not supposed to think or feel "that way" and block them or hold them in, you literally stagnate the energy flow, thus creating something similar to an energetic cyst, locking that thought or feeling in your system. Fortunately, that cyst can be dissolved, with the energy being re-assimilated into your system, so that things flow freely again.

A good example of this is an incident that took place in my office years ago when a client of mine came in for psychotherapy, as well as Energy Medicine. She had been to physicians throughout the country looking for help with unexplained pain throughout her body. No one could find anything wrong with her, regardless of the myriad of tests she underwent. We began making some progress with the pain while also helping her get some answers to things that were happening in her life.

After a month or so she came into my office for her appointment enraged. When I asked her what the problem was she immediately started sobbing. When she could speak, she simply said, "I hate my kids. I never wanted them, my husband did. Now I have 4 kids less than 5 years of age (twins and 2 single births) and he has a job where he travels and is only home on weekends. I gave up a job I loved for a life I hate." She continued to sob while she took out her checkbook to pay for her session. When I mentioned she had only been here a few minutes she said, "No one wants to be with a woman who hates children."

I then mentioned that I had two teenagers and could actually understand her feelings completely. It stopped her short. She stared at me and asked if I was telling the truth. When I mentioned that there was not a girlfriend in my circle who hadn't had a day or two of wondering what on earth she and her husband had been thinking when they chose to have kids, she sat there in shock. She couldn't believe people actually admitted that—and, furthermore, that they still had friends afterwards.

Her judgment on herself for being human, for feeling over-whelmed and unhappy, had been bottled up inside for years. When we discussed the possibility of her getting a part-time job, she was shocked that it was acceptable. She thought she was supposed to want to stay home. For those women for whom the domestic life is their dream, I wish for them the glory of the task. I did it for a few years and loved it even though there were moments when an adult, any adult, would have been treasured company, all while I felt blessed beyond words to have two exquisite, funny, gorgeous, healthy children. For this woman, things had been different.

I continued to see her weekly, and within two months, she was discussing the realization that each of her children had his or her own gifts and unique personalities—and what a wondrous surprise that was for her. How wonderful for all of them, that they could be appreciated for their beauty and uniqueness. She also mentioned to me that since that day in the office when she had sobbed and sobbed, she had not felt any pain anywhere in her body since. She wanted to know if there was a connection. There most certainly was.

To make a simple analogy, if you can imagine that every time she thought she hated her children, and every time she had a feeling of wanting to run away, she held that thought and feeling in because it was "bad," you can understand that she was creating more and more of these energetic cysts I spoke about. With all the other energy in her body that is generated every time she moves, or her blood flows, or a meridian or chakra functions, she has all this energy that, as it tries to flow through her body, keeps hitting these cysts that are stuck there. It becomes similar to the action in a pinball machine, and that new energy is bouncing off each cyst as it flows. No wonder there is pain.

By releasing all those thoughts and feelings, in a safe place and without being judged, she could finally create an energy balance in her system, one "cyst" at a time. She could finally stop judging herself, her feelings, and her humanity. What you think or feel is not wrong, what you do with those thoughts and feelings, however, defines whether they will support your health or not. By descending into judgment and self-hatred, and then putting that hatred onto all the others in her life, this woman clearly forgot who she was as an embodied soul and instead identified herself as a victim in an unbearable situation. Changing herself image changed her reality. Changing her reality changed her health.

By coming to understand and accept herself for who she was, she was able to live in her truth, rather than hating herself for the lie she was trying to live. She followed her own soul's longing to be free and productive outside the home on a part-time basis and thus could bring the joy she and her children deserved into the home. Her soul began to sing, and her body then began to dance with the joy and passion that she longed for. Everyone won.

Understanding both your stresses and how your body responds to that stress allows you to see the patterns you have developed over the years, based on how you hold your energy, how it flows within your body, and again how you react or respond to the events of your life. That understanding has an amazing ability to support you in taking your life back and in seeing that your life and your health are far more under your control than you realize.

Have you ever noticed that you were developing a slight headache from exhaustion and knew you should stop and go to bed or sit down to relax, yet didn't? Then you may have noticed that the headache was getting worse, and yet you "only had two more things to do."

A short while later you might have been close to tears, or nauseous, because your head hurt so much, and yet you wondered why this happens to you, and "why now?"

Recognizing that your body was telling you something and that your soul knew that it was time for self-nurturance, time to stop, long before you "only had one or two things to do," is crucial to your health. Not listening has a price. When you don't hear what is being said to you in a subtle message, the message tends to get progressively louder. You know what is good for you; you just don't always know enough to listen.

Come with me on an adventure into the real self, the solidly-connected and integrated self, the one you may never have known existed, or perhaps had a sense of but only occasionally encountered "by accident." It is so much easier than you think. Claiming the innocence of the child and the wisdom of the adult becomes an exciting way to do life and brings great joy.

To begin, discover what it is that you are here to accomplish. You know that when you see what fills your soul and body with excitement, with an eagerness to get up in the morning. What is it that makes you glad you are you? So many folks come into my office unaware of what feeds them, what excites them, or what makes them feel alive. For the most part, it is because they have lived their lives being who they were "supposed" to be to such an extent that they forgot who they really were. Learning to try new things or to explore potential interests until they found something that excited them seemed too difficult a chore for many, especially since they "should" already know, yet how could they?

As with anyone that you are getting to know, making friends with yourself just takes time. How much time it will take depends upon how invested you are in the relationship. Learning how your body energy feels when it is balanced versus how it feels when there is a problem in a certain part of your body is an amazing endeavor. You have lived with this body all your life, yet getting to know it inside and out, at any age, is an adventure of discovery because there is so much to learn. It supports your health and takes you along the path you came here to walk. When you are living, not surviving, your life, the energy flows even in difficulties and your journey is a process of unfolding.

I have written two other books based on how your soul speaks through your dreams and your aspirations entitled *Dreams Are Only the Beginning: Becoming Who You Were Meant to Be,* and *The Companion Workbook.* They are based on the premise that your soul speaks to you in many ways while attempting to unite the spiritual and physical worlds you are always traveling in simultaneously.

This is different than the body/soul connection in health, and yet it is not; you are simply listening to a different type of message. Your soul's longings for your journey, for doing what you have come here to do, is revealed in that desire from deep within for you to grow and move forward, to reach for the next dream. Each dream calls you to become more. Each builds on the other.

The message is subtle, and yet not. Listening to your body/soul conversation, hearing the song your soul sings, lets you recognize that you can hear and feel it all through you, in every cell, when it is time to go forward, when it is time to stop being comfortable and to grow again. Usually, it makes you feel restless, and you start to want more from yourself and more from your life; you don't feel at home in your body anymore because you are outgrowing your current way of being in your energetic body.

Learning to listen to that knowing sends you on the path of truly living the life you have come to live. Not for a moment does it mean you have all the answers; you don't even have all the questions. They come as you go forward, as you learn enough to question this next stage of the journey and to find your place in it. It is not a passive process; it requires your full commitment and a willingness to risk and to grow. From my experience, it requires a constant reaffirming of a willingness to take a risk, yet you know if you don't take that risk you will become more and more dissatisfied with your life and with who you are. After a while, it doesn't even feel like a choice anymore; it feels like a necessity.

Amazingly, you also need time away from this process—a time out—time to just assimilate what has happened and what you have learned. That can be a vacation, a night out on the town, or even an afternoon football game or movie. Anything that gives you permission to stop thinking and just play, just relax, and just laugh, is a much needed gift in the midst of it all. Those are the things that bring balance into your life. If you don't have that balance, you must find it. It is a necessity, not a luxury, if you are going to keep you and your journey in perspective and not take yourself too seriously. Time away from your "life" is a gift you give yourself... A very important gift!

This life is a wonderful trip; I do hope you enjoy the ride. I have written this book to share with you possible ways in which you may have betrayed yourself by living in fear, in defense, and out of touch with who you truly are, so that you can more consciously take those leaps, those risks needed, to come back to the life you were meant to live. To living your life in such a way that you allow your soul to sing and your body to dance, giving you greater health on all levels while living your dreams, your passion, and your joy!

CHAPTER ONE

Three Levels of Existence: An Overview

If all the conversations that you can recognize going on simultaneously in your life at this moment appear to be more than enough, prepare yourself, since there are even more. Clearly, the need for quiet, whether in meditation or during a long walk each evening, is real if you are to support your own inner peace and have the ability to continuously assimilate all that happens in your life inwardly, and in relationship to the outside world. You need the opportunity to catch up with yourself and each of the conversations taking place within you, as well as to assess whether your life as you are living it is supporting your growth or calling you away from who you truly are. Too many people in my office have realized that they have been surviving their lives by simply getting through each day one day at a time. They cannot remember the last time they felt alive or in touch with who they really are.

When you are able to assimilate what has been happening in your life on a conscious level, and you begin to feel at home in your own skin, there are various levels of awareness for you to acquire so that you can go even further into your own journey with a deepened sense of self-awareness. Of the three levels of existence, the Personality Level is the most superficial and unfortunately, the most conscious even though there is so much on that level you can still be unaware of. In Chapters 3 through 11, I will go through much of what that level entails in detail.

Beneath that level, in terms of consciousness, is the Hara Level, the level of intentionality. It is on this level that you make the decision to follow your intent or to live in self-betrayal. I will discuss this in more detail in Chapter 12.

Finally, on the deepest level of your existence is your Core Essence, your soul, which reflects who you truly are. This is the level you are called to live on as you progress in your ability to live from the truth of who you are. This is the real you. The Hara reflects your willingness to live in this truth and the Personality Level reflects how you have chosen to interact with the world around you.

Your soul has always existed and always will; therefore, on this level you have nothing to fear. If you have ever had a moment when you felt, throughout your body, that you were exactly where you were supposed to be, fully present in your life and in that moment, even if only for a second, you were experiencing the gift of truly coming into this place of truth. The level of the Core Essence is expanded upon in Chapter 13.

Learning to integrate all of this can be simplified a bit if you look at yourself from the perspective of being a multi-dimensional being where whatever affects one level of your existence simultaneously affects them all. It shows you that nothing about you can be compartmentalized as if it is hidden from the other levels of existence. Denial is the only thing that can give the illusion of compartmentalization but it is clearly an illusion. An example of how this works can make it a simple concept to understand.

Think of a time when you went along with others and did something you really did not believe in. You knew better, knew it was not a good idea, and yet you went along. You didn't feel good in your body; it just didn't feel right—not bad, just not right. You went against your own soul's knowing of what is right for you. That was your core essence, or soul level, giving you a message. As always, it was speaking through your body.

You felt ambivalent throughout the experience because your intentions were mixed. You wanted to support your friends, but it meant not supporting you. Your level of intent was now impacted, since it was not straight, or in alignment. Finally, because you did not feel good in your body, and your intentions were contradictory, you were not in the best of moods, and were probably quite defensive and reactionary. Now your personality level was impacted.

This is a simple, clear way of looking at how all of who you are is impacted by every decision you make. You are amazingly complex, and yet you are not. Every decision you make, impacts you multi-dimensionally. Hopefully, you can see how you can, without the intention, betray yourself so easily and create dis-ease in your system.

If you are very sensitive and conscious of not hurting others, you can betray yourself repeatedly. If you do not take the time to find out exactly where you want to go in your life, or how you want to get there, you can spend time in ambivalence, feeling progressively worse about who you are and perhaps settle into a life that was not of your choosing and yet a consequence of an unwillingness to take full conscious responsibility for your life and act according to where your soul was leading you.

You are unique, a unique package of skills, insights, personality, and vision that you bring to the world. As a result, you are needed because of what you can bring to the world. If you chose to live from your heart/soul connection, you would bring the gift of your essence to the world. Imagine if you stepped out of defense and chose to live in a place of unconditional love, recognizing that we are all in this together and that we are all part of one whole, each with a different sense of self, a different quality that is uniquely ours to help transform this world. For some, the soul's quality radiates goodness and kindness, for others, wisdom, and for others, clarity. Learning to see the soul's essence of another is a gift that delights and allows you to see the intrinsic holiness of that person.

As it exists now, there isn't one embodied soul out there you can't learn from. In addition, you have so much to teach but only if you are willing to learn. No one can teach if the student is not willing to learn, and no one can fully teach or lead if they themselves haven't first looked at their own issues and then claimed their place on this planet and their right to exist, on every level. That can be a challenging task to accomplish. All of you come from human parents, and live in a very human culture. There is so much blame, anger, and feelings of inadequacy that govern your lives that remembering who you truly are can be very difficult at times.

Some obstacles, or belief systems, can develop or be taught to you as a child that lead you to living in self-abandonment, self-betrayal, or self-sabotage. These obstacles, or defenses, all exist on the level of your personality. Amazingly, you have an unlimited capability to flourish and grow in ways you never knew were possible, while you also have an amazingly unlimited ability to keep getting in your own way. If you have ever tried to achieve something very challenging, you may have seen this happen more than once.

In my practice, I have frequently watched clients create large and small difficulties for themselves while simultaneously blaming others for anything that goes wrong in their lives. It is so much easier to point your finger outward, because that doesn't require change or the need to rethink your own actions or beliefs. Haven't you seen yourself or a dear friend do the same thing repeatedly while continuously hoping for a different result and blaming others when it doesn't work out the way they had hoped?

Working with all the patients and students I have, as well as with my friends and myself, has convinced me that humor and faith are the two most absolutely necessary qualities for getting through this journey. You need to be able to laugh at yourself first since taking yourself too seriously will cause you to lose perspective. You really are a wee bit crazy, but in the nicest of ways, we all are... It is also important to learn to connect so fully with others that you can laugh, without judgment, at their wee bit of craziness as well, since we all have some. With an ample capacity for humor and faith, you can begin to see that, usually, what makes your life so complicated and so painful is just you.

Understanding how we all create our own craziness or health may bring further laughter and lightness to understanding these three levels of existence and how to work with them to bring more of you into your life. Energetically, each feels very different and brings a very different experience of the self. I will begin with the most superficial, since that is the one that is presented most frequently and, ironically, oftentimes has little to do with who you truly are.

The Personality Level

It is here where much of your personal work begins, since this level is often who you think you really are, probably because it may be the level on which you are most conscious. It is the level you come from when you are in a reactionary mode. This level is continuously being developed, since it is the way you present yourself to an ever-changing world. This level most reflects your desire to be safe, or to be loved, and, accordingly, your personality develops to ensure that one or the other, or perhaps both, occur for you.

When I meet people, and I know what to look for, I can often quickly tell who it is that needs to be safe. Some show that need by instinctively taking control of everything and everyone, as if it is their right. Whether they do it with a smile, a sense of entitlement, seduction, manipulation, or intimidation, we all get the message; they want control to feel that they are safe. Your learning to observe others is an important skill in walking this journey. In doing so, you will not need to react; you will learn to respond, calmly, logically and with your heart open.

There are also those whose sole concern is not about controlling others, but rather about controlling their own lives and space. These people need to have everything perfectly set up and in order so that they can feel safe in their environment. Only then can they attempt to relax. Finally, in a search to feel safe, there are those who, rather than looking to control others, or their environment, decide to simply avoid the anxiety of living by losing themselves in books, fantasy, or distractions.

There are others who, on the Personality Level, are more driven by the need to be loved. They may try to achieve that by continuously asking for things, for attention, for time, and so on, as a means of being taken care of. They can appear to be very draining at times, yet being cared for is what supports their almost constant need to be seen and nurtured. If others give to them, or take care of them, they feel loved or wanted, at least for that moment.

There are also those who, in their need to be loved, will give themselves away completely. They may volunteer endlessly, believing that someone will see how good a person they are and then love or appreciate them accordingly. They may also look to others to define them. "Tell me who you need me to be and I will become him or her. Tell me what you want me to wear, how you want me to talk, or laugh, or what sports you want me to like. I will become what you need me to be, so that you can love me."

Whether your longing is to be safe or loved, it is translated into a focus and a personality style that is learned or developed as a child. As you grow into adulthood, your personality and your style may change slightly or significantly; that is entirely up to you. The degree and the way in which you grow, however, depends entirely upon whether you are searching to live in your own truth, connecting to the essence of who you are while living your life purpose, or, whether you instead live your life governed by your fears focused on the world around you, believing that "out there" you will find a way to feel safe and loved as a means of avoiding loneliness, feelings of abandonment, or fear. In the latter case, surviving is far more important than living. It is a choice.

If and when you begin looking inward and developing a level of self-awareness, the Personality Level is most often the first level you look at and analyze, because it is on this level that you try to fit in, to find your place, professionally and personally. Often this process begins when in your body you begin to feel the emptiness, the absence of so much more of who you are and what you want in your life, and in you.

The Hara Level or Level of Intention

This is the level that resonates with you when you purposefully chose to live your life in a particular way, when you live in response, rather than reaction. To live on this level, there must first be a sense of awareness of who you are and how you fit in your world. At this level, you are much more capable of living in intent to support you on your journey, to make your dreams come true, or to avoid the self-abandonment, self-betrayal, or self-sabotage that can exist on the personality level. You are able to live on this level when you have connected to yourself sufficiently enough to know what it is you want, what it is you are dreaming about, and who it is you really are, even as you are in the process of becoming.

It is on this level that you are clear, focused, and aware, with an ability to live in contentment, and self-honoring. The power of this level is demonstrated when you witness the ability of those who practice the Martial Arts and the amazing feats they can perform. To do so, they first learned to be in intent, to be focused solely on what they were doing in the moment. Their feats could not occur, and certainly not with the fluidity and ease that is required, if they were distracted, in self-doubt, or ambivalent.

Part of their training is in the discipline of being focused and in alignment with their intent of the moment. When you are living on this level, things are just what they are, and you can accept them accordingly, dealing with all situations and people for who they are without the tendency to go to reaction or judgment, either of the self or of others. The intent is to be fully present, to accomplish your goal, and to do it with ease, naturally. Imagine the peace in living that way.

The Essence or Core Level

To the extent that you have come to understand and accept yourself, and chose to live your life in a grounded intention of being responsive to others and to life, rather than reactionary, you have learned to live from the essence of who you truly are—the undefended, non-reactive, and spontaneous self. At this level, you are the purest self you can be. This is a place where unconditional love is a way of life and a way of viewing the world. From here, you live a life of joy, lightness, and choice rather than one of sadness, heaviness, compulsion, or reaction.

On this level, there is a detached, and yet intimately connected, understanding of life, of the journey, and of infinite wisdom. Authors such as Maya Angelou so beautifully present this level of being in their ability to have energy, peacefulness, and an understanding of existence far beyond what is usually seen. This core, or soul, level reflects the infinite soul that has always existed and, as a result, reflects your unique self with all the gifts you possess. It contains the compiled wisdom of all the journeys you have walked. From this level, you can honor your humanity, while also seeing the infinite, unlimited qualities of your soul reflected through your heart's ability to love unconditionally.

It is worth remembering that, as embodied souls, you possess all of the best spiritual qualities imaginable, and, as a human, not only do you possess the ability for unconditional love, but you also possess the other aspects of your humanity that make you cringe, and, at times, wonder what you were thinking. Hopefully, this combination allows you to have enough spiritual detachment, even from yourself, to have the humor, faith, and wisdom needed to walk this journey with grace and unconditional love.

It is important to remember that you are never "done," that you will never be the illusionary "perfect," and that, while you are still walking this path, you will continuously be confronted with greater challenges, calling you to claim more and more of the truth of who you are. That is a gift—not a failing.

Life itself is an endless process of unfolding, and, yet, somehow it offers you an exciting, overwhelming sense of joy, accomplishment, and freedom. I know that for me, each time I face another challenge, each time I take another risk to grow, the experience of letting go of what has trapped me or held me back occurs. I end up feeling more alive, more vibrant, and more me than ever before. Nonetheless, risks still cause me to catch my breath, pray, and hope I am not totally crazy, but rather being led to grow a bit more.

Thankfully, I have met people along the way who were at home in their bodies, who felt at home in their lives, and at home with themselves. They became my mentors and guides. It has been in observing them that I have come to understand how our spiritual existence/connection is reflected physically.

They were at peace; I could see it. They radiated. They still had difficulties, as we all do, but they were of no consequence in their minds, and would be dealt with. Those folks are the angels each of us are given along the way. They will remind you when and if you go off track simply by being themselves and doing it in a way that makes it looks so easy.

As best I can, I would love to do that for you here. My journey has been amazingly varied, with more adventures than so many will ever know. Still, the discovery of the mind/body/soul connection has been a gift beyond words for me. Being traditionally trained as a psychotherapist, I never thought I would work in the field of physical health, yet, as I continued my studies, I moved into the field of complementary, now called integrative, heath care.

During the course of that training, I recognized gifts I possessed to see things I hadn't realized could be seen. I literally started seeing the energy around people's bodies, and, when I got over that shock, I realized I could see the energy within their bodies, as well. Eventually, as I became more comfortable with these developing realizations, even more skills unfolded. I came to recognize that when you let go of your hesitations, there are unlimited abilities you possess regardless of your area of expertise. The issue, as I see it, is much more about a willingness to surrender the illusion of control and of what is possible, and simply allow things to unfold. That is much easier said than done, I realize, yet the rewards are amazing.

For me, what became most rewarding was that I developed the ability to be with someone and sense who that person was at his or her core level. The fears and the gifts s/he possessed became easy to see as well. When you can see someone that intimately, that wholly, it is easy to recognize how lovable s/he is in the pure, undefended state and you cannot help but see them that way with the rest just being their "stuff." It has changed all my relationships, professionally and personally. Professionally, that letting go has brought in experiences I never thought possible.

An example occurred many years ago, on the first Friday night of a new class I was teaching. I had asked a student to lie on a massage table so that I could demonstrate a particular healing technique I would be teaching the group that weekend. During the demonstration, when I was directing my attention around her abdominal area, I saw something, and asked how she was feeling. She said, "Fine, although the doctor says I have bladder cancer and it may have spread to my ovaries. I am having surgery on Monday."

Clearly "fine" is a relative term. After taking a deep breath and becoming very present to the moment, without distraction, I went to the level of intent and focused much more specifically on that area of her body. I saw, and sensed, several tumors on the bladder. She actually had 18 very small cancerous tumors on her bladder, yet they had not penetrated the surface of the organ. When I looked to see the ovaries, I saw that they were clearly in an environment that was very cloudy, similar to a room filled with smoke, yet they were not cancerous, simply unhealthy from the environment they were in throughout the abdominal area. I told her she indeed did have cancer but that she would be fine.

On the following Tuesday, her friend, who was also starting the class, called to inform me that this student indeed had 18 tumors and that they had all been removed and her bladder saved. She also said that the ovaries were not cancerous. I am always thrilled and in awe when something like that is validated. I know it is real when I see it, yet having it validated is one more way of knowing I am not "crazy". Thankfully, we do come to accept our gifts, but the validation is a luxury, not a necessity. For me, it is now just as rewarding to be able to spend my day showing people a strength in their personality, a connection to their soul, and the opportunity to live at peace in their life. It brings such a sense of completion that that is my driving force.

Giving hope and joy to those without it and hopefully providing the opportunity for a moment of self-love to those who are prone to self-judgment and self-hatred makes my day. I am a born optimist and I love to laugh, a good, solid belly laugh, and the thought of bringing laughter and inner warmth to those without joy makes my life worth living. Helping others achieve that soul connection, letting their soul sing, is work I treasure.

Laughter, unconditional love, and safety provide the background for your inner work, while you begin to see who you truly are, and see that your major problems usually are self-created and easily resolved if you are willing. Taking risks is the only real way to make changes in your life. I truly believe that life is simple, it just isn't always easy. Look to see if you have a well-developed ability to make your life complicated and convoluted. A clue may be that it usually results in your feeling overwhelmed and victimized. Think about that.

If you do that, understanding how you do it can, if you are willing to make changes, make room for you in your life again, so you can start leading your life, rather than having your life lead you. You can become the leader in your life, rather than the reactor, simply by stepping out of that dynamic you have created. Remember, on the level of intent, if you are here to live from your essence, you must be willing to look at the ways in which you lose touch with who you truly are. That may mean, at times, looking at the ways in which you get lost and then finding your way back home.

It's when you stop to notice how you feel in your body, when you experience what it feels like to simply stop, that you are reminded of the "you" you have forgotten. I have heard clients say, many times, some version of "I lost me along the way." In truth, as an embodied soul, you can never lose yourself along the way. What you can do, however, is lose your connection to your core essence, to your soul, along the way. That happens when you get so lost on the Personality Level, so engaged in your defenses, that you cannot find your way out of the confusion and/or the pain. Developing the life skills needed to find your way "home" after getting lost is a blessing you deserve.

As I said earlier, much of this book is focused on the Personality Level since that is where we can lose our connection to self. Through case examples, I hope you can identify your personality style and how it helps or hinders your ability to be present in your life and, as a result, soul-connected. I begin next by addressing the various aspects of the Personality Level, your wounds, your fears, and your defenses. Then, in following chapters, I go into detail about each personality style with numerous examples from my practice and from television characters. Remember to look for yourself on these pages, rather than looking for and judging the others in your life! Laugh, be empathic, and enjoy!

CHAPTER TWO

The Personality Level: An Overview

I have included a figure on the next page to show you in visual graphic form the levels of your existence including, in more detail, the several components of the Personality Level. Notice that when you are in reactionary mode, you disconnect from your true essence and become caught in a revolving cycle of mask, defense, lower self, wound, and core wound with no escape. For some, it is a life style, while for others you may go there when you are frightened, tired, anxious, or depressed.

Because so much of your reactionary energy comes from your intense will, at those times you can become caught in passion, obsession, or the need for control. It is very difficult to stop and get to a balanced place in order to step out of the cycle. Finding what works for you, what trick or trigger you can develop for yourself, to get you out of that momentum is imperative. Finding a way to not get caught in the first place is even better.

You will learn that the much more powerful, balanced level of intent is far safer, feels so much more real, and actually gives you a far greater sense of yourself and how to get what you want. It is not at all about will but rather is a gentle, powerful focus of intent supported by your very essence. You will come to see that intent and will each feel very different in your body. One flows freely, the other holds on, oftentimes for dear life.

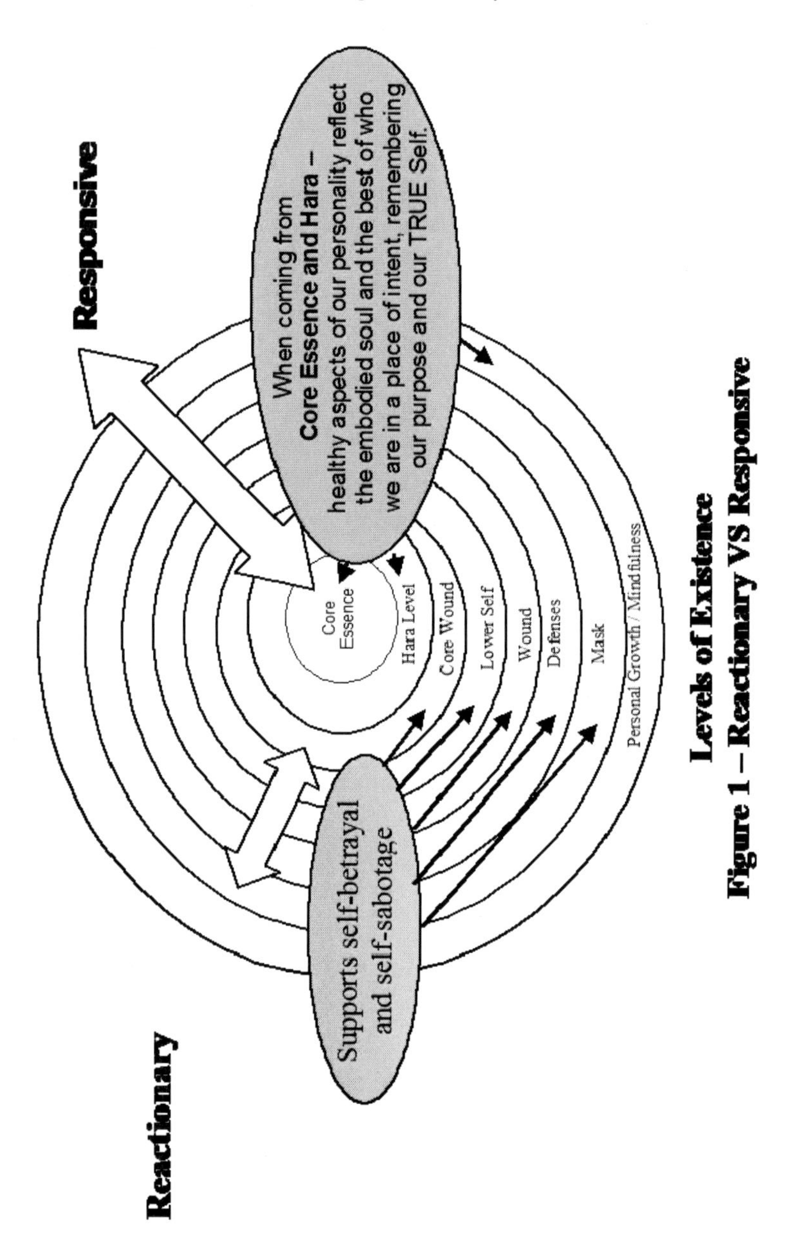

Levels of Existence
Figure 1 – Reactionary VS Responsive

Remember, your spiritual, emotional, and physical health are impacted greatly by how easily your energy flows. Happy people rarely get ill; it is those who are stressed and troubled who are most vulnerable. The reactionary side of this figure demonstrated for you a visual image of those layers of your personality that most affect your bio-field in terms of holding energy or creating points of stagnation, deficiency, or excess.

Your body is naturally meant to be free-flowing, balanced, and at ease, as shown on the right. If you are holding onto thoughts, feelings, or beliefs because you are filled with judgment, whether of yourself or of others, your bio-field becomes congested and, if not treated or cleansed, diseased. Since I will discuss each of these layers in detail according to your personality style in the following chapters, mark this diagram page if you like, so that you can easily come back for the visual.

The outermost rim of this figure shows you specifically where you need to begin if you are to bring joy, passion, flow, and change into your life. Once you become conscious of what aspects of you and/or your life you want to change, you can then begin to claim ownership for who you have become and who you want to be. Take pride in all the things you love about yourself; take credit for having chosen to become the person you are. You had choices to make and the ones you made created the you that exists right now. Then take a look at the qualities you don't like about yourself – we all have them. Perhaps, they are comments that you repeatedly say but wish you could take back, perhaps beliefs that keep you stuck, or emotional reactions you no longer want.

In this adult state of consciousness, you will begin the journey inward, through personal growth. You will learn to see the mask, the defenses, the lower self, the wounds --small and large – and how they are impacting your life. Finally, underneath it all, you will come to see your ability to live in powerful, gentle, focused intent that makes it possible for you to reclaim your passion, vibrancy, and joy as you move forward to the level of the real you, the essence of the true self. Your heart will open and your passion will come alive simply by making this a full-bodied decision. You will feel it in the excitement of coming alive during the process; there is no need to wait until you "got it."

Your mask, that image you want to project to others, exists because you don't believe the real you is sufficient or good enough. You project the image you were taught to project so that were considered to be correct or appropriate. As a result, that image becomes more important than the real you. For many, the real you gets forgotten. It gets lost because the focus remains outside rather than within, focused solely on the other rather than the self.

Your defenses come up when you are in fear, and your focus is on the "other" and how s/he or they may serve, love, or control you. Unfortunately for some, their whole life is lived being fear based. The world is seen as dangerous and people are seen as the enemy who cannot be trusted. Certainly there are dangerous situations and people who have chosen to live out of integrity, but our lives are lived on a spectrum of love/trust and fear/hatred. Where on that spectrum you live is your choice and based on the filter through which you see the world.

Your wounds exist as a result of what your experiences have been and how you have perceived them. One experience can deeply wound one person while having little impact on another. Some have lived horrific lives, yet appear to have far less damage than another whose life has been fairly stable and loving. Regardless of the severity, wounds usually come from feelings of rejection or betrayal. How wounded we become, and how frequently we are wounded, is often our choice.

We all go to those places of fear or wound at times, yet some people live there much of their lives. If this is you, there is a whole new world and world view available if you are willing to take a few risks and grow. Getting caught in the cycle of mask, defense, and wound, keeps you disconnected from the truth of who you are. You can get lost in the illusion of hopelessness and/or powerlessness. As a result, the decision to grow is not consciously fed and therefore does not call you to take the risks necessary to give up the struggle and come alive. It is only when you become so uncomfortable and realize that you don't want to do your life this way anymore that you take a risk to change it.

I have noticed that whenever you decide you are ready for change, real change, things happen; the openness helps you notice the opportunities in front of you. Because you are open, I believe that Spirit, or the universe, or whatever you choose to call it, makes things available as well. It is as if the world has been waiting for your consent, a choice made from free will. As soon as it is acknowledged, everything that was standing still starts to move. Always there is your free will and at any point in time you can change your mind and attempt to stay stuck again. Yet when you grow, when you take the risks needed to move forward, you quickly run through the illustration on page 16, going from a choice to grow to coming from your essence.

You are then able to more fully achieve what it is you have come here to do. What it is you have come here to accomplish for yourself and for the world around you. It seems to me that you have a very personal purpose in your life, to learn to live in your truth and bring all of who you are to the forefront. I believe as well that you are here to help transform the planet and all those on it. If you follow those tasks, and the risks necessary to make them happen, you are fully living this life, not surviving it. All of that is a choice. A choice made consciously or unconsciously, but a choice nonetheless.

Personal growth, a by-product of recognizing personal responsibility for creating the life you want, calls you to look at yourself and the people in your life, without judgment. This isn't meant to be an arduous task, but rather an adventure of self-discovery allowing you energetically to feel freer, lighter, and more alive every step of the way. If you make all this a heavy burden of misery, as some do, based on a belief system that life is a struggle—and perhaps an uphill one at that—it will be. Remember, it isn't what happens in your life that defines you, but how you deal with what happens in your life.

I believe that you are meant to live this life vibrantly, passionately, and with all of who you are ready to come out at any moment as needed or wanted. How many people never really live before they die? How sad. I am fully aware that I speak from a bias of having fully lived this life of mine, and I would do it all again. I started my life in a home for children, was later adopted, and moved to the housing projects. Although I was a good kid, after-school detention was not an unfamiliar experience for me. I could tell you that none of it was my fault, but I have a vague memory of at least a few things I did that may not have been my smartest moves.

After initially planning to get married right after high school, I decided instead that I wanted to become a social worker. Since the school I attended in South Boston was not accredited the necessary higher education for such a career was not readily accessible for me. Not to be deterred, I decided to become a Catholic nun, since they did social work. After a number of years in religious life, with a different name and different clothes, I was able to get a college education and do social work. A dream was fulfilled, and I found a me I never knew existed; perhaps that is why I want to share the opportunity with so many others.

When I knew, on a soul level, that I was meant to leave religious life, I found a new dream, and, shortly thereafter, I moved to Manhattan and became an international airline stewardess. That was only the first 22 years… I share this with you to show that I truly do believe you need to live this journey. You need to follow your dreams, and, to do that, you most importantly need to get out of your own way, take risks, and come alive. Life is such a gift when you are living it, but a burden when you are surviving it.

If you can think of those moments that are not your finest, or that keep you in fear, anger, rage, or illusions of fragility, realize that the more of those emotions you hold onto, for whatever reason, the more congested your system gets. Forgiving others and letting go of your need for revenge and/or victimization supports your health. You may be justifying making others pay for perceived wrongs, but you are paying the higher price. In addition, the more you stay on the Personality Level in mask, defense, or wound, the longer you are preventing yourself from flowing freely from your own essence and allowing your passion, joy, and peace to flourish.

Ironically, it is the Personality Level that becomes your greatest ally in living who you really are by using all the skills in your personality available to support you on the journey. It is also on the Personality Level that you may instead choose to survive, rather than live. You know the saying that you are your own worst enemy or your own best friend? This is the level that makes that decision, consciously or unconsciously. Learning to be body-aware significantly increases the chance that your decisions will be far more conscious than not. A wonderful side-effect is feeling great and healthy in your body, as well.

Clearing up that congested energy is far easier when you let in a new thought or a new perspective and allow your energy to begin flowing again. That has been the objective of psychotherapy. Another solution can be found in talking to a friend and actually listening to what he or she has to say.

Another great way to get energy moving is through exercise, in whatever form you choose, because that also causes your energy to flow; it gets things moving. It eliminates stagnation naturally. Have you ever noticed that once you can get yourself up off the couch and start moving, things just seem to look and feel better? What a gift, and it is simply another great reason to exercise.

If you become attuned to your own body, you will notice areas where the energy seems stagnant, where you feel dead, perhaps, in contrast to other areas of your body that may feel flexible, or alive and energetic. Noticing how you feel in your own body, how the energy flows, allows you to understand what is happening on levels far deeper than your consciousness, and that level of knowing is a great tool for self-awareness.

From the perspective of a practitioner, I am aware that when I hold my hands over a particular block, I can quickly feel what emotion is held in that block. If I hold it longer, I can begin to sense, see, or "know" what the experiences were that created that emotional holding pattern. If there are several experiences repeatedly held in that one block, I can begin to identify them. Years ago, I got a call from Australia, from a man who had gotten my name from a referral list of energy practitioners.

He called to tell me that his doctor was considering surgery for a back problem he was experiencing, but that he wanted to try energy work first, hoping to avoid surgery. I told him that he should hang up while I worked with him and call me back an hour later. After I hung up, through the Hara Level of intent, I initially scanned his bio-field to see what I could discover. I saw, or sensed, something in his lower back that was out-of-sync with the rest of his back area. It felt different. As I looked closer at this particular area, I was able to sit in silence and simply experience that part of his back as if he were a client sitting in my office.

As I sat in his field, I saw a vision, or a movie, in which I saw a young boy of around four years of age fall from a tire-swing in his front yard. When he fell, he felt "stupid," as if he should have known how to swing in a tire. His belief (an energetic reality) in his "stupidity" got locked in the area of pain he had from the fall. When that same self-judgment comes up in his adult life, guess where it is going to hurt him... Not surprisingly, there were a couple of other incidents in which he felt "stupid" and simultaneously felt locked and pained in that area. In that hour I was able to balance his back and other consequential imbalances that had occurred as a result similar to a domino effect.

When he called back, I asked what was happening in his life at this moment. He told me that he had devoted 11 years of his life to a particular company, but that it was now closing, and that he felt stupid for having taken a chance on new product development in joining this company when it first began.

He couldn't understand why his back was hurting him, since he hadn't fallen or done excessive exercise recently. When he understood that this was the location where he held the belief in his supposed stupidity, and that he was feeding an existing blockage that began when he was 4 years old, we were able to support him in changing his belief system to one where he could see that, rather than being stupid, he was a risk taker who took challenges to grow and get ahead.

Through no fault of his, the economy was changing and the company was closing. He had enjoyed his time there, had loved the adventure of a start-up company and all that he had learned. Now was simply the time for his next adventure—one he could undertake with great thought and a willingness to take on a challenge, which was something that had always excited him. Releasing the block, balancing the field, and following that up with a belief system change, so that he did not support a reoccurrence, permitted him to put this behind him and move on.

Physical problems are, in actuality, the final symptoms of issues that began ultimately on the spiritual level. If they are not resolved on that level, they move to the emotional level, and, if not resolved there, they present through energetic blocks, or cysts, as energetic, and ultimately physical, irregularities.

Physicians are well aware that the emotional frame of mind of a patient undergoing surgery impacts the ability for the surgery to go well, as well as the patient's ability to heal. Knowing how to direct that mind-set provides you with the tools for a healthier, more vibrant, and more passionate you, whether with full health or with the ability to live with whatever chronic emotional or physical imbalances you may have while living the journey, rather than surviving it.

Healing Ourselves

Three of the more commonly accepted tools, such as prayer, meditation, and rituals, all serve to support you in remembering the spiritual dimensions of life. They are tools for the journey to inner silence and reflection, as well as necessary steps if you are to live from your essence, rather than from a reactionary style.

In addition, the ability to understand what is happening in your body, as I said above, to be able to understand your honest, and immediate, reactions to things and to others, comes with an innate ability to understand and accept who you are, without judgment. So many of us judge ourselves according to who we have been taught we should be, and how we have been taught we should feel.

Permission to accept where you are, what you feel, and what you think about something changes everything. You may not always choose to act from those places, but understanding what is going on in them allows you to see what your truth really is at the moment.

That chance to look at yourself and accept where you are (remember it is not who you are, simply where you are), also gives you the chance to recognize that perhaps you need to stop; you need a break. Perhaps you have been pushing far too hard and for far too long. Simply by observing your behavior or responses, which may or may not be out of character, you get to acknowledge, first hand, that some self care needs to take place, and soon.

In my years of working with clients, patients, and students who were searching for a way to understand themselves while also living in relationship with others, I have come to see 4 progressive steps that are necessary to go through in the quest for healthy bodies, healthy relationships, and a more vibrant, alive, and satisfying life.

These steps take work, if you are used to not being actively involved in your own life; you will need to be nurtured as you explore them, so that they can come to be enjoyed and used as steps for growth and not steps to support self-hatred or self-judgment.

1. Self-Awareness & Personal Responsibility:
   - First, learn to identify your own personality style, traits, and tendencies.
   - Then take responsibility for your behavior patterns including all your reactions and responses.
   - Acknowledge that you are not your behavior.
   - Understand that behavior is a by-product of conditioning and choice, conscious or unconscious, but choice, nonetheless.

2. Relating to Others:
   - Observe how you respond or react to different people and personality styles.
   - How clearly do you hear what they say?
   - Do you already "know" what they will say and have a prepared reaction just waiting for a chance to be expressed?
   - Do you judge before you know the truth?
   - Do you know what fears you have in relationships with others?
   - What do you want in a relationship with others in your life?
   - You need to know what you want and from whom in order to get it.

3. Heart & Soul Connection:
   - How deep a connection do you want with others?
   - Are you interested in a life of intimacy?
   - If so, are you willing to let another truly see you, letting that person see the "good" and "not so good" aspects of who you are?
   - Are you willing to give up the masks you wear to project yourself as something you wish you were?
   - This step presents you with the opportunity of truly being seen, being loved completely for who you are, and, most importantly, loving yourself as you are at this moment.
   - This is absolutely necessary for a deep, fulfilling relationship.

4. Co-Creation:
   - Finally, when all the above has been addressed are you willing to own the reality of co-creation?
   - Can you acknowledge that you have never walked alone and that your life is a result of the opportunities presented and of the choices you have made?
   - When you look at your abilities and the choices you have made in your life, can you can see, without judgment, that at times you have made choices based on emotions, on imaginary need, or in haste?
   - Can you accept that sometimes you have made very good choices, but those choices were not meant to be forever, such as a job or a relationship? They were gifts you gave yourself that lasted as long as you needed them, even if not as long as you may have wanted.
   - Taking responsibility for your life gives you the freedom to sit in your truth and look at what it is that you truly want to do with your life, and to make the decisions necessary to make it happen. It supports you in living your life in focus, in intent, and with assertive ownership, rather than with passive acceptance.

This progression through your journey, allows you to understand that to be free to live the life you want, the life you came here to live, it is imperative to remember who you are, why you are here, and what it is that feeds your soul. You will be blessed with many dreams for life, and for you, all of which help you become whole. The gift is in the journey, in those you meet along the way, and, always, in the discovery of what makes you "you," while progressively understanding the strengths, abilities and perspectives you didn't know you had. Through all this, you continue to learn to love, to find joy, and to take the risks needed to let your soul sing and your body dance in all that you are. Now, let's look at where you begin or continue the journey.

CHAPTER THREE

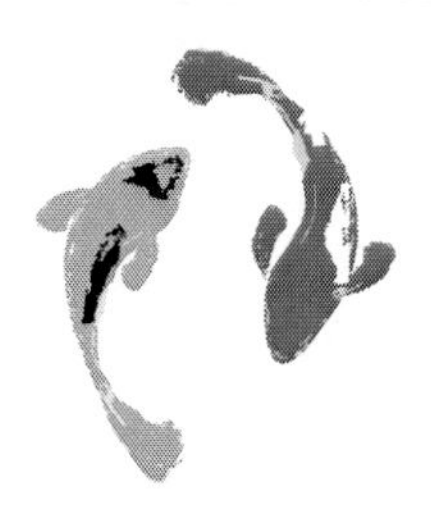

Personal Growth and Mindfulness

Personal Growth:

Personal growth itself is not a choice, really. How you grow is where the choice comes in. The reality is that you will grow; you simply have the option of deciding if you will grow in a way that supports you, or grow in a way that makes your life much harder than it needs to be. We make it much harder when we find ourselves continuously getting into the same predicaments and then blame all the folks in our life for the mess.

"If only they were different, my life would be so much easier…" Do you really believe that is true? Could it be that, no matter who was in your life, you would blame him or her? If you want a different life, or a different experience in the life you have, what are you willing to change? What belief system? What perspective of yours needs to shift in order to have difference in your life? What world view?

I have found with many patients and students that a belief that life is a struggle causes them to struggle with everything they do. If they believe that life is hard, the first thing I tend to hear from them is how hard things are. My question is always, what are you willing to change about you? In what way are you willing to grow? Amazingly, "they" whom we habitually blame will seem to be getting it only after we decide to grow and change ourselves.

Once we stop the blame game and give up the illusionary victim role, once we are ready and willing to take responsibility for our lives, becoming whatever we can dream, we are then ready to begin the process of personal growth that supports us in coming to a place of co-creating the life we want.

Going forward and backward on this is only human; accept your humanity in the process. It is fun to grow when you see the immediate results. Imagine, however, what happens when you can no longer blame someone else for your being late? It also means you own responsibility for everything you do wrong or avoid doing; that part is not always fun.

This conscious choosing causes you to participate actively in your life. It puts you in the adult consciousness and truly allows you the freedom to create a life you can be proud of and that you can claim as your own.

However, when you don't consciously chose to grow, life seems to move away from you; you lose touch with others and ultimately with yourself. You then end up changing as a reaction (if you change at all) to being left behind by all those who are more actively involved in directing the change and the growth in their lives.

When you are ready, following your soul's longings, listening to that inner voice, takes you to places that you might never have chosen, and to places that support your natural evolution rather than where you may have gone if you had just used your head. Your heart and soul take you to places far greater than logic can accept, but only if you listen, and then act. Life is far too short for regrets, so I believe in following your heart. That does not mean irresponsibility or chaos, as some may fear, only a conscious choice to follow your heart and soul and know, as best you can, the price and the responsibilities involved when you do.

I have found that, often, the price is in changing a world view—expanding it far beyond what it had been previously and letting go of the illusion that you had things figured out. What you get in taking those steps are gifts far beyond anything you ever could have imagined. It means taking risks and jumping off a lot of cliffs in your lifetime, but I know that for me, there isn't one risk I wouldn't take again.

The laughs, the joy, the sense of freedom, and the sense of self you will achieve are worth every bit of the fear, the sadness, and the occasional loneliness that are also a part of it all. I truly believe, as I have said previously, that too many people are surviving this journey, not living it. Grow with it, change, and discover a new way of life. Even if nothing external changes, you can.

Many of the incoming students in our school speak of a need for something different, something that will support them in growing and in finding that part of them that got lost a long time ago. They speak of a need to find a place for themselves in the world. They usually want something that supports their passion, their vibrancy, and their absolute desire to be really here, to be a part of the world and to be seen for who they are, not just for what they do.

They are choosing to grow, even though they are aware that they do not necessarily have any idea as to what that entails. What you can learn is that when you make that choice to change, whether because the way you have been doing your life no longer works for you, or because you have recently had a major change in your life as a result of divorce, a broken relationship, a death, a job loss, or even your last child heading off to school, things will require you to do your life differently.

The common issues that arise are self-hatred or self-doubts. More often than not, in those pivotal moments, you see things in yourself that you realize you have been avoiding. You believe that you alone have secrets to hide and things that "prove" you unworthy of succeeding or of being loved fully. You see issues you felt you had worked on years ago, and here they are again, alive and in screaming color. You recognize pain that you are still carrying. In recognizing all this, in risking to actually see it all, you are being given the opportunity to now really deal with it.

Those things that you have avoided confronting—such as feelings, beliefs, responses, or reactions—do keep coming up. If you deny that they exist, they tend to show up underhandedly. If you deny you are angry, it tends to come out in a way that will sabotage you, perhaps in passive-aggressiveness. If you deny you are frightened of an impending opportunity because of the changes it will require, as well as frightened of not getting it because it can open up new worlds for you, there is a good likelihood that you will either not go after it, or not be fully present in the pursuit.

Mindfulness

Mindfulness, a requirement for this personal growth, means just what the word says. It implies that you are aware of what you are doing and mindful of the choices you are making, in each moment, as a way of life. This state of living requires you to be conscious of where you are, whether you are in your truth or in self-betrayal; it requires you to be aware of what you are saying and the impact your words are having both on yourself and on others. When you are mindful, you are not able to practice denial.

A great benefit of this is that, as with anything you do often, you can, over time, develop an easy passage into your core essence. When you leave it, and go into defense or fear, coming back to your truth can become progressively easier, just as, with your lawn, you can create a path simply by walking often enough over the same area. You can also, with a practice of mindfulness, create a very familiar path to get to your core when you realize you are not there.

Finding yourself capable of such immediate contact with your core implies that you know yourself well enough to know what you are feeling when you are feeling it. Do you feel as if you are "beside yourself" at times? Are there times when you feel as if your life is running ahead of you and you can't catch up? Do you have times when you feel you are outside of the picture that is your life, as if you are watching it? Do you have moments when you know you are not being real, yet you don't know how to get back to the real you?

During those moments, if you are mindful, you are conscious of what is happening with you. Because you are conscious, you have the choice of deciding whether this is how you want it to stay or if you want to change the energetic experience of your life at that moment and become more actively involved and participatory in your own life. At one level of growth, you don't realize when you are out of your truth; you think this is what you or your life is like. In a state of mindfulness, you are aware when you have left your truth and realize it is not you, and you know how to quickly get back to the essence of who you are.

Coming to know yourself so well can actually be quite exciting. It is like reading a book where you are discovering a whole new world, a whole new you, with unlimited options for change and growth, if you want them. It is also the place where you begin, as you progress in your path to living in your essence. The first logical step to being able to discover you is in looking at the masks you may wear without even realizing it. Removing those allows you to put your focus on the real you, the "you" you will see in the mirror.

CHAPTER FOUR

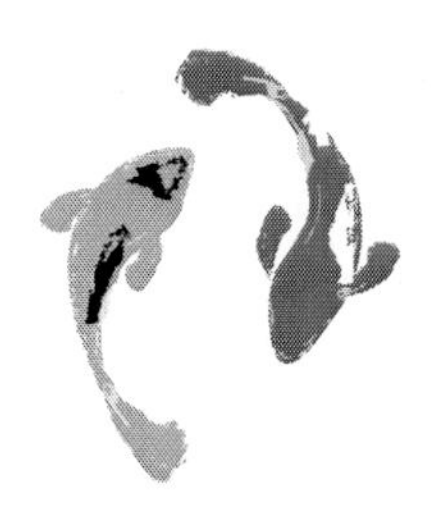

The Mask

Many of you want to believe that you are "real," yet have forgotten, if you ever knew, who the real you actually was. As an example, if you were raised to believe that you were supposed to be a "good girl" or "good boy," you learned early that you are praised, or even loved, only when you are good. As a result, being "bad," as we all can be, required not being seen by others when you wanted to get out of that shell. Many of you learned to be "naughty" without getting caught. For others, acting out meant doing it with great rationalizations to yourselves so that even you didn't need to see it as bad. It was, or is, a great way not to have to own a side of you that you would judge harshly.

Most of you have known people who present as the sweetest little thing to the public, and yet you have seen the other side that comes out on occasion. Haven't most of you been exposed to that person who has on such a strong mask of "good" that it is clearly unnatural, and so sugary and sweet that it can become annoying? The individual in that case needs you to believe that he or she is that good because, as a child, it was his or her way of being loved and appreciated—and who doesn't need that? He or she is most likely not even aware of the impact that presentation is having on you, since s/he has been living with it for his or her lifetime. S/he may not even see it as a "presentation," but simply as who s/he is.

There are many other masks, as well, far too many to list. It is also important to note that the same mask can look very different on different people with each having a slight difference in the qualities. Using the "good girl" mask as an example, one woman may always be overly sweet and kind and as a result never says no to any request so that you never really know if she actually wants to help or just does it because she believes she should.

You will come to feel uncomfortable asking for something because you do not know if she will resent it even though she agrees, or if she really wants to be a part of something and is thrilled. Another woman may always anticipate other people's needs and do things to support you that you never wanted, and now you feel obligated to enjoy or participate in something even if it is an inconvenience. These are different qualities of the same "good girl" mask yet each feels different and each can encourage a different energetic response. Although there are many more, I will share a few examples:

- If you were raised to believe that you were supposed to be very intelligent, your mask may be one of superiority. Not having an answer or being seen as wrong is considered a crisis and that can't be allowed to happen.
- If you were expected to be strong, you will put undo stress on yourself to be able to handle all sorts of physically challenging tasks to prove your point, or take on or endure emotionally challenging situations to show that you can handle anything.

You could also have one of these masks:

- Spiritually evolved, so you are "above" feeling emotions.
- Kind and saintly, with no connection to any other part of you.
- Delicate or emotionally fragile.
- Powerful and threatening to show you have no fear.
- Altogether to show your perfection.

Knowing your mask, or masks, gives you the ability to see where you leave the truth of who you are in order to become who you were "meant to be" according to others' expectations and demands. These masks developed when you were little and were taught how you should be perceived by others.

The Irish have a saying that, "You wash your dirty laundry at home," meaning that only the best face can be shown on the street. What this does is make it impossible to ask for help or to find a way out of a possibly horrible situation, for fear that you will be judged if others know "your dirty laundry."

It is believed that, under all circumstances, the mask, or presentation, is what becomes important, not the needs of the person or the people behind the mask. You can get lost in the presentation and, unfortunately, if you use it long enough, you may lose your connection with you as a result. I have had a number of patients tell me that they were frightened that if they dropped their masks there may be nothing beneath them. What if they found out there was nothing to them? No soul! No essence! No real them! That is an unfounded fear, but real to them, nonetheless.

I once worked with a woman who told me she only felt nice emotions. She only felt good things and could never understand why others felt anger or impatience, since she never did. I also worked with a couple in marriage therapy who were having some difficulties. When I asked each what most made them angry with the other, the wife told me that in 32 years of marriage, she had never once been angry with her husband.

Never once! She wasn't lying to me, she was lying to herself. Her husband felt she was mad often, but wouldn't talk about it, so they never worked through anything. After 32 years, although they still loved each other, there was a serious problem now that the kids were gone and he wanted a more real relationship.

I do not want to say that you should never wear masks, only that you should know when you do. If you are enraged with your boss, but the two of you are on your way to a meeting with clients, it would serve you well to wear a mask long enough to let the situation go temporarily, knowing you will deal with it later. Recognizing the problem and the need to deal with it allows you to honor what you feel, plan an effective way of resolving it, if possible, but then put it out of your mind for the moment to join as a team to do what needs to be done.

For a few brief seconds, you may have had to wear a mask when you really felt like another look would have been far more real. The difference is, when it is a choice, when you are conscious of yourself on many levels, you are far more connected to that embodied soul, and perhaps will even get a deeper, more satisfying solution to the problem because you stepped out of the way and could be open to more options, later.

When the mask is denied, you are invested in maintaining all of your energy on the level of personality. Think of what that does to the energy flow in your body, as well as to your ability to connect with the truth of who you are.

Take time, if you are willing, to look at your life. What masks do you wear? How often? What motivates you to do so? If you don't see any, do you have a friend you trust, one who can be honest with you without fearing your anger or loss of the friendship who might help identify them for you? What does he or she say? Can you believe it? Can you see it?

What I think is most important when you choose to grow is that you give yourself permission to be human. Many students I have worked with judge themselves so harshly for being human, for being "unfinished." It is as if not being fully "perfect" makes them defective.

We are all in process; we are all on a spiritual journey, learning to live from our essence, our embodied soul. Imagine what the world would be like if we all lived from the essence of who we are rather than from a fear that we are not good enough. There would certainly be the realization then that we are all in this together. What we can do at this point is recognize that if we are consciously trying to grow and are "not there yet," perhaps we can have far more compassion for those who are "not there yet" either.

Your parents have certainly influenced you, and helped define your world view; yet, once you reach 18, you achieve your young-adulthood. You are then the one who makes the decisions about your life. Your parents told you not to eat before dinner, yet do you munch as you cook or even eat munchies while you are figuring out what to eat? Were you told not to talk to strangers, and yet your life is filled, in business and in service, with speaking to strangers.

Without realizing it, perhaps, you let go of the messages that no longer fit how you want to do your life. You let go of the limitations that were imposed upon you when you were a child, at the same time choosing to keep other messages, such as, "You will never amount to anything." "That is too hard for you to do." "You're not like the others." You may even hang onto the message, "Don't get too big for your britches."

This tendency to hold onto unproductive patterning seems to be due to the fact that either you are not even aware that your parent's pronouncements are still running your life, or you still hold onto the imprinted belief that they are right.

Can you see how believing that is in fact buying a mask that doesn't fit? "You will never amount to anything" is a statement made by a parent who either knew of no other way to get you motivated, or who had no idea of who you truly were. If you want to amount to something, you will. You must first give up the mask of failure, or incapability. You have to give up all those belief systems that have you stuck and release all that energy to achieve that you have held back in order to live out the messages imposed on you. Moving all that stagnant energy throughout your body helps you in remembering that you are so much more than even you realize.

What does your heart want you to do with your life? What is your soul calling you towards? The best way to know is to look at what feeds you. What makes you feel most alive? What is it that would make you want to rush out of bed in the morning? What are your dreams? I truly believe that your soul calls you to become what you are meant to be through the dreams you have for your life.

If you notice, when it is time for a change in your life, so many things in your life seem to feel ill-fitting all of a sudden. You notice a sense of restlessness and a need for something different. I believe that is the soul's way of saying it is time...

Listening to that is learning to listen, again, to the soul as it speaks through your body. You already know so much about what you need and what you have come to this earth to do. You simply need to remember. Have you ever had that experience where you know it is time to grow in a certain way or to do a certain thing, and yet everything in you seems to be blocking the way?

When you finally get out of your own way, things just work out so smoothly, almost as if you had planned it that way, or perhaps as if you had help all along the way. Letting go of all the images of who you were supposed to be or not supposed to be, allows you to be open to what is and simply be who you are.

I believe that when you finally commit to making a decision, and go forward in living your life, Spirit gives you the opportunities you need to go to the next level. It is your choice whether you take them or not. Spirit is there, but you are also required to participate. Praying, opening up to them, and working to have a miracle makes it possible to notice that job posting, or that stranger that "just happens" to cross your path.

I believe miracles take place every day. Your spirituality, the recognition that you are an essentially spiritual being, is a very pragmatic, intellectual, and profound aspect of your life and one that gives your life its greatest meaning, direction, and fullness. It is on that realm that you are most fully you, without any need for mask, perfection, or safety, while the love from others is the gravy.

Can you now see the difference between being in mask and being in your truth, admitting who you are and what you feel—to yourself and to another? Because there is no pretense, you naturally flow through each of the emotions that comes up, releasing them as they appear, without judgment. Your body stays balanced, regardless of how many or how strong the emotions are, since they are permitted simply to flow through you as they arise.

It is when you put on your mask or go into defense that you complicate the journey, as well as compromise your health. Being human, you go in and out of fear and all the means of self-betrayal possible. The difference is, when you are consciously walking a path of personal growth, you visit those places of mask, defense, wound, and core wound. When you are in self-betrayal as a way of life, you live there.

The choice to be conscious and out of mask not only gives far more joy, it also allows you the ability to deal with things as they arise, so that you do not have to carry them in your body for long periods of time. It becomes clear how being spiritually and emotionally healthy supports physical and energetic health and balance. What a discovery that was for me as I walked my own journey, as well as supported so many others in walking theirs. It certainly makes psychotherapy a far more spiritual and physical experience than I dreamed it would be from what I was taught in graduate school, and a far more growth-producing experience than many patients realized it would be when they began their therapy path.

The greatest reward in all of this is that, in learning to live from your core, rather than in mask, you learn to live in a place of unconditional love. You are able to achieve that level of relationship that allows you to truly know yourself and another, and to see the beauty in both of you. This is where true intimacy exists, true acceptance, and not in spite of who you are, but because of it.

There are no bad guys here, only folks who choose to live in their truth and come from their essence, and others who choose to live in defense and fear, and thus in self-betrayal. Remember for a moment those times when you felt most connected to someone. It is usually when you have felt most seen, and most accepted. How wonderful to know that you are seen, accepted, and loved because of who you are, not for who you are supposed to be.

All the dimensions of who you are get seen, those parts of you that are all loving and kind, or clear and concise, as well as the tougher parts of you that want revenge, love to be spoiled, exist to be self-righteous, and/or need to be in control and demanding what you want when you want it. As an embodied soul, you have the traits of both aspects. Accepting that and knowing it allows you the freedom to look at what you love about you, and relish it.

It also allows you to see the parts of you that you don't like, that cause you embarrassment, or that betray who you really are, keeping you stuck in a place you have long outgrown but haven't yet been able to let go of. Accepting all this allows you to love you, and then others, equally. This is the true win-win situation, and you are capable of it, if you are willing to pay the price and to look for, and live, the real you in the journey of your life.

CHAPTER FIVE

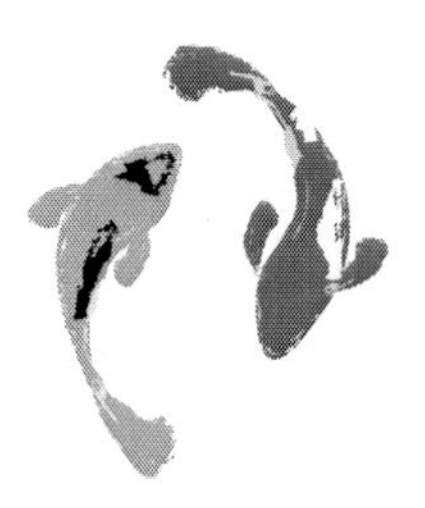

Character Structure Overview

There are as many theories of the human personality as there are theorists; as a licensed psychotherapist I have read or learned many of them. Some of them are fairly outrageous and judgmental, from my perspective, and some of them can be well-intended but lack some of the fullness that I believe is intrinsic to human nature, such as our spiritual essence. Still, others are very informative and useful. Each one, however, helps us acquire a developing perspective of humanity since they build on one another, or cause us to explore further what makes us who we are, while gaining perspective on how we relate to others and to the world around us.

In my experience, the theory that best encompasses all of how we are and that is fairly simple, although not simplistic, is the approach developed by John Pierrakos M.D., a psychiatrist and colleague of Wilhelm Reich. He called his approach Core Energetics. This is a favorite of mine for many reasons, although most specifically because of the emphasis on love as a driving force and on energetics. My experience with clients, patients, and students is that this approach is the most pragmatic and most easily understood; consequently, it is the one I share regularly.

Pierrakos taught that we each have five personality styles, or character structures, with each of us having a tendency to emphasize one more than the others, defining our uniqueness, gifts, and vulnerabilities. The character structures discussed in Core Energetics reflect our highest qualities, as well as the defensive reactions we utilize when we go to fear rather than love. They show the traits we possess within each character structure and that we can use either to support our journey or to sabotage ourselves. For additional information on these structures, which we will discuss shortly, I recommend a wonderful book entitled *The Undefended Self* by Elizabeth H. Michel. The objective of Core Energetics is in learning to live your life in love rather than in fear, learning to come from the essence of who you are rather than your defenses.

Understanding and working with the defensive component of your character structure, as well as understanding why you go into defense, gives you the ability to accept those parts of yourself you don't like or want. Seeing defenses as the reactions of a wounded child allows you to be compassionate with yourself while moving further into the strengths rather than the fears of your structure.

Finding what supports you in living from your essence and in love rather than in fear is the gift you give yourself, and that discovery also helps the journey become that much more rewarding. Learning the tools that work to bring you out of fear, and out of defense, so that you can live your life fully and with love, laughter, and faith, is a gift not just for you but for all those you touch.

If, by walking into a room, you can have the ability to calm or enliven people as needed—to remind them of the joy of living, of the gift of the human experience—simply by being real and abandoning your habitual defenses, isn't it worth the effort? I truly believe that on some level we all want to make the world a better place and that there is a part of all of us that wants to bring peace to those we meet. You may not always connect to that part of yourself, but it is still there; even if you choose not to hear the conversation between your body and soul, it is still happening.

Coming to understand your character structure in the process of your personal development, and claiming it, you will grow to the place of an individuated ego, developing an independent sense of self while recognizing your unique gifts, talents, and vulnerabilities. These make you different than, and yet still similar to, all others. Once you have achieved that healthy sense of separateness, you then evolve to a point of realizing that, in actuality, we are all one. Not only are we all in this together, we are all one. We breathe the same air, we walk into each others' energy fields, and we are greatly impacted by the "other" simply because we all exist here, together in this same space.

If you are going to live in peace in this connectedness, you first need to notice what you do that destroys that connection even when it is your intent to stay there. Because there really are, at the base level, only two emotional starting points, love and fear, you need to learn to notice when you go into fear and what you do at those times so that you can create other options of behavior and/or inner responses to support connection with yourself and with others simultaneously.

The first place to start is to begin to notice when it feels as if you are in defense. Have you noticed those times when you have said something and then realized that wasn't you; that wasn't who you wanted to be? It came out of you but it was so unlike how you would have wanted to respond, or even how you truly felt. That happens when you do not respond, but when you react instead. As difficult as it may be to hear, what you feel and do in such a situation is a choice—a process that requires reconditioning, perhaps, but, nonetheless, they are a choice, and are part of a behavior pattern that can be changed.

Learning what you do when you go into fear, understanding how to respond differently, and wanting to, are really all that it takes. We truly are not victims of our behavior, only illusionary victims of our upbringing. If there are patterns within your behavior that embarrass you, change them. If there are responses that you say and then regret, learn to develop a new "norm" in response. It is at those moments when you feel you are not really saying what you mean, what you want, or what makes you comfortable in your own skin that you are in defense.

That feeling of discomfort in your own skin is your soul's way of saying, "Come on home; remember what you know to be your truth." It is uncomfortable in your own body when you leave the truth of who you are and take on another's energy, or abandon your strengths and go into fear.

In understanding the character structures, both the strengths and the defensive patterns that they entail, you can easily begin to see that certain responses or reactions are not "you," they are simply elements of your personality, the most superficial aspect of who you are in this lifetime and they are, if you choose, changeable. You are not who you were ten years ago, or twenty years ago. Life has shown you that change was needed if you were to reach your goals in a new environment or a new context, so you changed.

If you got your first job, you changed; you got a better sense of responsibility and independence. If you got married, you changed; you learned a lot more about blending and compromising, and that changed you, or you learned to fight harder to get your way, and that changed you. If you had kids, you changed; you learned about putting someone else first, about the need to give, while also taking some time to live.

In looking at the personality structures discussed below, notice that each has traits that support a balanced and healthy flow of energy throughout your body, opening the pathways to free expression of your essence, and each also has patterns of behavior that support self-betrayal and the closing down of energy flows, cutting you off from your essence, as well as negatively impacting your ability to sustain or achieve physical health in specific ways. We all possess all five of the structures I will discuss.

The percentage of each of these structures present in an individual makes a significant contribution to the variations in our personalities. Some may be 70% of one and 20% of another, with the final 10% scattered amongst the remaining styles. Others may be more evenly balanced amongst all five.

There is no correct combination, nor is there one correct way to do your life. You need the strengths of each structure. It is the unique blend that is yours alone; the combination of the package and the flavor you add is what makes you interesting.

Your natural gift in spirituality or your natural gift in building community, in calling others together, or your natural tendency to love and support others and see the best in them, or to be chosen as a leader when you least expect it, or to organize and be the responsible one of the group, are each strengths that exist within the various structures. Whichever gift is most naturally yours, it reflects the unique strengths of your essence, of your personality, and your structure. It is the gift you brought to the world.

At the school, on the weekends in which we teach each of these character structures in significant detail, we have had students who wished they had more of this personality style or that, as if one was better than the other. That is a false assumption. Each structure offers you necessary tools for living and becoming whole.

It is important to remember that you need those who can see the big picture and are spiritual in nature; those who are empathic community builders; those who are powerful, strong, and loyal support staff; as well as the leaders and the organizers. You need to develop each of these skills within you, those that come naturally as well as those that require more effort. The combination allows you to experience all of who you are on this journey. Developing them can also cause a lot of tears and a lot of laughter as you recognize the many things you haven't quite conquered. Not taking yourself too seriously is an important trait to develop along this path of growth and forced humility.

There is so much more to each personality style than we can provide here as we will be providing only an overview or taste of the richness you possess, a richness so worth knowing.

CHAPTER SIX

Creative/Schizoid

Creative/Schizoid Overview

Healthy Characteristics

- Sensitive, extremely perceptive
- Spiritual, often psychic
- Brilliant, innovative thinkers
- Imaginative, creative, artistic
- Good at understanding the world symbolically
- Can easily grasp the big picture – not getting caught in details.

Unhealthy Characteristics

- Existential fear – constant
- Persistent anxiety
- Can be hyper-vigilant
- Need to develop boundaries in claiming their space and their right to exist
- Not present in daily living – often losing or misplacing things – accident prone
- Can be oblivious to what is going on around them.

Relationship Styles

- Non-invasive
- Non-confrontational
- Can be very intriguing and intellectually challenging
- Avoids closeness – remains aloof and distant
- Suspicious
- Emotionally vulnerable.

Basic Beliefs

- I am safe if I am invisible
- If I become fully present and alive I could be in danger
- I don't fit in here
- I feel disconnected even from myself
- I can't trust my body or my feelings
- There's something wrong with me.

Common Illnesses

- Muscle and ligament disorders
- Skin disorders
- Bone disorders
- Joint or neck problems
- Anxiety
- Schizophrenia.

Creative/Schizoid Structure:

The wound of this particular character structure traditionally presents itself in utero or at the time of birth.There is a clear belief that the world is a dangerous place to be in. Consequently, the energy pattern of this structure supports a stronger connection to the spiritual world and/or theoretical thinking patterns, and, as a result, there is possible resistance to being present in the pragmatic, day-to-day realities of the physical world.This lack of presence is demonstrated in so many different ways, such as the tendency to lose keys or eye-glasses or not remember a conversation or a meeting that took place just a short while ago, including who they talked to during it.

There tends to be an existential fear, even a terror, that exists within this structure.The fear is not necessarily directed at any particular purpose or event; it energetically exists throughout the body simply as a consequence of needing to be in the body to function even minimally. Learning to surrender and relax, trusting that they are guided and protected, would be a real gift they gave themselves if they could only do that. Unfortunately, if this is an extreme part of your personality, you are easily overwhelmed by the ordinary day-to-day tasks of living.The absent-minded professor is an example of this type. Does that describe you?

My father used to say of these folks, "He may be smart, but he doesn't have a brain in his head." It always made me laugh, but I understood his point. Of course, Dad was a sheet metal worker for years, who later became a policeman; both roles required a great deal of awareness of his surroundings, so his approach to the world and those in it was dramatically different from that of a professor who could deal with theories and principles. This latter style can readily stay in the realm of theorists and researchers without needing to ever get overly involved in the application of their theories on a daily basis.

Also, because of their connection to the spiritual realm, those with this structure can have it as their second-nature to be mediums, psychics, and/or gifted healers; conversely, those with these gifts tend to have this as their primary personality structure. If this fits you, your ability for intuitive knowing or connecting to those in the spiritual realm comes easily because you have a stronger connection to the spiritual world than to the physical. Your 7th chakra is wide open more so than for others. However, depending upon your next strongest (secondary) character structure, you may also have a great ability in applying this knowing to support a very pragmatic spirituality.

Having employees with this as a primary structure can also be a real asset to an organization because of their ability to think out of the box and to see the big picture, for the moment, and for the future. These individuals are your visionaries and your artists. Unfortunately, for many of these visionaries, because of their corporate success, they are often promoted into positions that require the implementation of these visions under the supervision of those implementing the vision. Neither of these, pragmatic, detailed positions fit this personality and, as a result, failure can occur; it becomes the Peter Principle in action.

As with all of these structures, in addition to the gifts that support you living at the highest level of your potential, there is a defensive aspect to each structure that supports a unique means of self-betrayal. The defensive aspects within the Creative/Schizoid structure deal with the difficulty in becoming so embodied that you experience your essence, something very difficult for those with this structure to achieve because of the existential fear.

When you are strongly defended, you have the tendency to not be present to such an extent that you may not be able to retain what is said or remember commitments you have made, making it difficult to rely on you for follow-through. Your ability to remain aloof or distant can make relationships difficult when your partner seeks a closer, more intimate, or connected, relationship with you.

The absent-minded professor and the mystic both fit well here. Their worlds tend to be more global than personal in nature, so you see the difficulty they can have in personalizing their journey. The propensity for global orientation is demonstrated further in the tendency to use the expressions "**All** of us" or "You **always** do." It allows you to stay invisible and to be safe. If "we all" do it, then it is easy to blend in and be safe, again without claiming your individual thoughts or beliefs, which would of course differentiate you from others.

Another expression of this structure is with those defined as "klutzes." Their lack of presence to their environment causes them to walk into things or trip over things that aren't there, or lose their glasses or keys regularly. Remember, we all have at least a touch of this structure (e.g., How many of you have walked into a room to get something and, by the time you are there, have not a clue as to why you went there?). If I may say so, this aspect also shows the need for humor and for friends who can laugh with you, keeping all of this in perspective, while you laugh at your own touch of craziness. For those for whom this is their major structure, much of the spiritual work needed is to connect with the self as an individuated entity. There is a need to claim your physical place in your life and in your relationships. Claim boundaries and the right not to share everything that is yours, or to keep certain secrets to yourself, and even make your time your own. Learning to say "NO" is a great gift – it helps you from needing to hide.

Characters such as Phoebe from "Friends," Kramer from "Seinfield," Professor Trelawney from "Harry Potter," the Scarecrow from the "Wizard of Oz," and many of the roles Jerry Lewis used to play, demonstrate the defended component of this structure, where the individual is not connected to the depth and essence of who s/he is as a solidly embodied soul. If you look closely, you can see their innate goodness, but often you need to look beyond the scattered presentation.

Others, such as Albert Einstein, Ghandi, and Stephen Hawking personify the strengths, creativity, and ability to think out of the box, out of accepted realities, and to open the minds of others to so much more than was thought possible. They truly believe that "because it has never been done before" is the reason to go for it, rather than the reason to not try.

When students present with this as their primary structure, they tend to forget when their homework is due; they may forget which weekend they have class, even though they are given a written schedule with the dates to help with organization and planning. Students with this structure, initially, can have great difficulty feeling the energy flow in their own bodies, as well as in the bodies of their classmates during healings. Once they do become present, however, they bring a wonderful wisdom, loving patience, and a much needed gentleness to their work. In addition, they bring the richness of their spiritual awareness, and the joyful physicality that comes from the body-connection to life.

The folks who have difficulties with migraine headaches traditionally present with a Creative/Schizoid tendency. Whenever I ask what was going on at the point of onset, they often tell me that they felt a subtle pain beginning, but they had a few more things they needed to do before they could look for their medication. When it got a little worse, they started getting anxious, because they knew what was coming and how bad it would be if they didn't stop, yet.... Finally, they are in a panic, their headache is getting worse, and they now feel nauseous and frightened. When I ask if they could have done anything to stop or prevent it, they will tell me, "No." They will justify this in saying that they have had this problem all their lives and perhaps their parents did, as well. From their belief, it is solely a physical issue and therefore nothing could be done. That is one way to avoid responsibility for their health and to avoid differentiation and the need for pragmatic self-care.

Perhaps they learned, since childhood, that things needed to get done, planned, or figured out before they could do self-care? As I see the pattern energetically, if a woman is 5'5", her head is approximately 6"–8"; the rest of that height is in her body. When we try to over-think or over-analyze our life with a belief that thinking or understanding is what keeps us safe, we end up attempting to hold all of the energy that belongs throughout our body solely in our head. There is a belief that, "If I can figure out this problem, or what to do with this situation, it will all work out right."

In reality, it may not make any difference, and yet, rather than tuning into our soul's knowing, we try to figure it out with a far more limited knowledge base, our brain. In going to sleep when a headache is that bad, we have the opportunity to stop thinking and allow the energy pattern to go back to normal, throughout our entire body.

When sleep is not an option, and I have patients with every type of headache in my office, I put them on the massage table. As I touch their toes, I have them lie quietly, bringing their focus to their feet, and simply experience the sensation of touch and warmth. It forces the energy out of their head and causes them to send their awareness to something physical and at the opposite end of their body. As I soothe their feet and warmly comfort them, they are soothed into experiencing their body and letting go of the obsession with thinking. It gets them grounded and present. From this grounded position, they are far more likely to find a solution to their problem or their worry than when they were in their head.

Although I am discussing headaches, I believe that this is true of so many of our soul's messages that we are given but do not necessarily receive, regardless of our character structure. Tuning into our body's experience teaches us so much on many levels. In addressing the Creative/Schizoid, however, what I have seen in my practice is that, on a physical level, this personality style tends to be more vulnerable or fragile. There is a tendency for these individuals towards bone, joint, and skin disorders when there is an imbalance in the system.

Their prevailing lack of attention to their environment can be a contributing factor to the injuries that can happen frequently, and usually on one side of their body—either the right or the left. Their skin, muscle, bones, ligaments, and tendons are what support them in being in their body, so, obviously, as they ignore their body as much as possible, there is a price to pay in breaks, sprains, cuts, and bruises. Have you ever discovered a major black and blue mark while in the shower and yet have no idea how or when that happened? You walked into something and yet "no one was home," so you did not feel the pain. I had been on the phone with a patient who mentioned, absent-mindedly, that she just noticed blood on the floor while we were talking. When I asked her to find out where it came from she told me she just realized her foot was bleeding. I had her hang up and deal with her physical needs. Teaching her to be present was a part of my task in working with her. The next option for her, of course, was to choose embodiment and live her journey fully, with the gifts of the structure and the ability to walk in both worlds, consciously.

As I have discussed, because of free will, you do have the option of not listening to the conversations between your body and your soul. However, because this is a spiritual journey, the spiritual aspect of your life is what governs the trip. You will eventually get the messages you need to hear. The real question is, when are you going to hear them? If you have noticed, with little ones, when they ask or tell you something, if you don't listen, they will simply keep repeating it at higher and higher decibels until that is all you can hear.

From my experience, and that of my patients, students, and friends, it seems to me that that is exactly how Spirit and our soul work, as well. When you get a subtle message and you ignore it, the next message isn't so subtle. If you do not hear that message, it will continuously get louder until you have no choice but to stop and listen to what it is you need to hear. Your soul may be telling you to stop and take a break; it may be telling you to stop and notice your surroundings, or to stop and come home to you, your body, and your inner knowing. Have you noticed that, when people get sick, they often say, "This is about the only way I would have stopped"?

I have had cancer patients tell me that, although they would not wish it on anyone, the cancer also gave them a gift. It forced them to stop and reevaluate their lives, something they have known they needed to do, but either they couldn't find the time or they were afraid of what they would find. I have had AIDS patients tell me that they feel as if they are living their life for the first time; they are no longer drifting, but have a purpose they are proud of.

Sadly, some people see illness as a punishment for something they have or have not done. Some see it as something that just happens to them from out of the blue while they were minding their own business. It isn't either. Disease is not controlled by the outside and dispensed as a punishment, and disease is not random. If everyone in a room were to be exposed to someone with an infectious disease, not everyone would be infected. The curious question is, why? What is the variable that causes some to be infected and others to remain healthy?

Deepak Chopra writes of cancer and its treatment, saying that Ayurveda is said to place the responsibility for disease at a deeper level of consciousness, where a potential cure can be found. The real culprit, as he sees it, is the persistent memory that created the cancer.

Candace Pert writes of Elmer Green, a Mayo clinic physician, whose work has revealed results showing that every change on the emotional level is accompanied by a change on the physical level. Candace states that neuropeptides are directing your attention, and that, although you are not consciously involved in deciding what gets brought to attention, you do have the ability to bring such things into consciousness and to process everything or most of everything that comes into your conscious awareness.

Richard Gerber, M.D. writes of the emotions' subtle magnetic energy that affects our physical health. He states that wellness requires an optimal balance of the energies on all levels—physical, emotional, mental, and spiritual. Louise Hay and Deb Shapiro have each written of very specific emotional and spiritual correlates to physical disease and disorders in varying detail.

For someone of the Creative/Schizoid structure, it is when they become physically conscious, physically aware of their bodies, that they can best come to understand their own health. They will begin to connect what was happening in their life at the time of onset of any disease with what imbalance may have existed emotionally and spiritually at the time. With their spiritual gifts, their ability for healing is increased greatly.

By understanding their personality, and structure, or yours, if this is your primary structure, as well as observing any reactions to life events, you will begin to see, without blame or fear, how your spiritual beliefs and emotional responses to them affect health in so many ways. It presents the power of health, whether in supporting its fullness or understanding the depths of the spiritual messages it brings if it means living with a chronic condition, as a gift calling you to a journey of self-care.

CHAPTER SEVEN

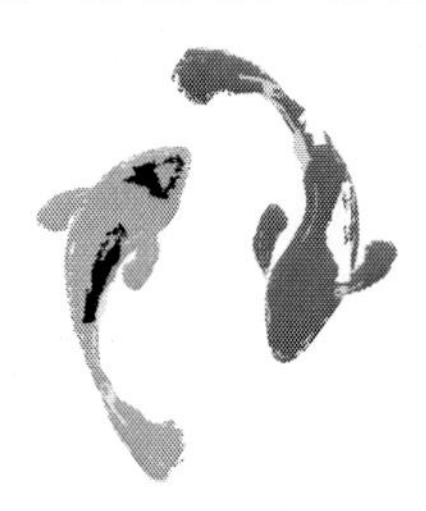

Empathic/Oral Structure

Empathic/Oral Overview

Healthy Characteristics

- Interested in others/empathic
- Tuned into other's needs
- Easy to trust – non-threatening
- Relates easily to others
- Good in the helping professions
- Expresses feelings easily, except for anger.

Unhealthy Characteristics

- They long to talk, especially about themselves
- Often do not know what it is they want, specifically
- Sense of entitlement, expecting others to fill their needs
- Material matters are rarely important, although, in the other extreme, they can be hoarders
- Tendency toward depression – feel powerless in filling their own needs
- There is never enough time, money, attention, etc.

Relationship Styles

- Can be very empathic and understanding
- Very joyful, with easy laughter
- Can be compassionate community builders
- Jealous
- Low energy investment
- Wants to be taken care of.

Basic Beliefs

- Everybody is going to leave me – I will be abandoned
- I'm all alone
- I can never get enough
- I need support
- I want to help others
- We are all in this together.

Common Illness

- Low immune system
- Reproductive issues
- Diabetes
- Lower back pain
- Addictions
- Obesity, Eating Disorders

Empathic/Oral Structure:

The wounds of this structure present themselves around the time of breast or bottle feeding. Some of the child's needs may have been met but not others. As an example, they may have been fed, but not nurtured. Examples of this that I have seen are when mothers put their baby's bottle on a pillow so that the child gets fed while the mother does other things. The child's physical needs are met, but what about the emotional and spiritual needs? What about the sense of bonding that provides the 6th sense connection between mother and child? Neither the mother nor the child is being fed in the full natural conditioning of this feeding process. When the mother holds the child while bottle or breast feeding, there is a feeling of safety, of connection, of being cared for that permeates every cell of awareness on so many levels. When only the physical needs are met, the child is left alone, without that connection or that sense of safety that comes from being enveloped in someone's arms; something we all long for at times.

This young child can grow up still searching for that experience of being held and being cherished, something they deserve. More than once over the years of teaching in the school I founded, I have held a student, an adult woman, in my lap and simply soothed her while I continued teaching and working with other students. They all understood that, at that moment, that little one was in the pain of her childhood wound and she was finally being given the opportunity to feel safe, soothed, and cherished in a way she never was. More than once I received a note being told of how life-changing that experience was, of how touched she had been after she got over her embarrassment, and how she was now able to let go of old pains that no longer defined her, making her current relationships so much more healthy. It takes so little to heal an old wound, when the timing and the conditions are just right.

The energetic pattern within the folks with the Empathic/Oral structure is very low energy flow throughout their system, which secondarily supports them in feeling powerless. It is a cycle in which, once they feel powerless, they then also have low energy, which makes them feel powerless and on it goes. They become the young child incapable of feeling their own needs and looking for others to do it for them.

Whatever the reason, the message received by the children with this as a primary structure was that their needs would not be satisfied, or perhaps not satisfied on their schedule. For some children, this is a non-issue, and they will adapt in a healthy way; yet, for people with this predisposition, this wound leaves them feeling abandoned and/or deprived. Consequently, when they are in the defensive state, believing their needs may never be met, they have the inclination to hold on very tight to anyone who comes into their life, often resulting in the new person feeling drained and overwhelmed and eventually moving on, leaving this individual feeling that yet again they are abandoned and left behind. This becomes a repetitive process. Give up the illusion of good guys and bad guys and you can understand both perspectives. Needing to be someone's "everything" is exhausting. Believing you need others in order to feel whole and satisfied makes you very needy for others to come and stay around, and to stay physically close. The co-dependency in the illusion of desperately needing them creates an unhealthy pattern of relating, and does not support either partner in growing or changing as nature requires.

On occasion, the new person leaves when s/he feels s/he has nothing left to give. Unfortunately for people with this structure, the experience of abandonment will be repeated throughout their lives if they develop a pattern of draining those they are in relationship with, since they will ultimately be left again, without ever realizing that their true needs could have been met, if they had identified and addressed those themselves, or had been more specific about what it was they wanted.

I once had a friend whose boyfriend called her, literally, 16 – 17 times per day from work, to catch up and say "Hi." If he missed a call, she felt threatened and misplaced and went through a great deal of pain because of a belief that his priorities had changed and her importance in his life had lessened. Thankfully, for her, he had actually never felt so needed, and thoroughly enjoyed calling, unless, of course, work intervened.

Because this wound occurred in a preverbal stage, many with this structure may never have learned to verbalize their needs and yet expect others to meet them. No matter what their partner does, however, it will never really be enough. Those who have this as their primary structure need to learn to identify their own specific needs and to take responsibility for getting them met. They need to learn, as well, how to feel filled in and of themselves. It is an emotional and physical experience they need to have because it proves the belief in their personal inadequacies to be wrong. Our belief systems become our reality. To change our beliefs, we need to have and accept an alternate reality. In this case, one that shows they are more than capable of identifying and filling their own needs as desired. They then become capable of choosing a partner because they want them in their life rather than because they need them in order to survive.

Learning that others in their life can be expected to support them but not to carry them is a great lesson for independence and freedom, and counteracts a means of self-betrayal in believing they are inadequate or powerless in respect to filling their own needs. Because, in the unhealthy state, much of their focus will be on getting their needs met by others, or on the wounds that occurred in childhood, there is little focus or ability to look within to find their own much needed strength, along with their essence.

Learning to recognize their strengths and their inner conversation allows them to live the depth of the journey they are walking, while connecting to a full joy that comes from their own heart and soul connection. In this structure, a life task is to recognize their needs and fill them, and, when necessary, to ask others for support along the way.

I had a couple come into my office for therapy after 10 years of marriage. He said that he wanted to be appreciated in this marriage, and that he wasn't. She said she wanted to feel loved, and that she didn't. When I asked what he needed in order to feel appreciated, he mentioned that every Friday night for 10 years he has brought home flowers to his wife, and that she just dropped them on the counter while they had dinner. I asked why he continued to buy them under those circumstances, and he mentioned that his father had been doing this for his mother for over 35 years, that they were still as much in love as when they married, and he wanted that for himself and his wife.

When I asked her why she would do this, she told me she hated flowers. I asked if she had ever told her husband this, and she said, "No, if he loved me he would know." This is a classic set-up, guaranteeing that her needs would never be met and she would have someone to blame.

He supported being set-up in that he never explained to her what this meant to him, or how much he loved her and wanted to show her, weekly. He also left himself out of this relationship in not sharing the hurt, but only the frustration. She never knew the depth of his longing for their couple-ness and connection, exactly what she was longing for as well.

I asked her what she needed to feel loved and she said she wanted to start every weekend with just the two of them, going out to dinner. The rest of the weekend could be running all over, but she would know he started it all with her. When I asked if she had told him that, she again said, "No, if he loved me he would know." For both of these individuals, there was a great difficulty in verbalizing their needs and, consequently, in getting their needs met.

Although they may have been wonderful contributing adults in many parts of their lives, in this aspect they were still living the wound of the child who could not identify its need and speak it, to ensure that it could be met. They didn't verbalize their wants and desires, and yet blamed the other for not fulfilling them.

Television and movie characters who portray this structure in their roles are Jake from "Two and a Half Men," George from "Seinfield," Ross from "Friends," and Mrs. Weasley from "Harry Potter"—roles in which they demonstrate the defended component of this structure, in which their needs are never met, or are not met sufficiently. Oprah is an example of one who comes from the strength of this structure, in that she discovers, nurtures, and fills the needs of others as a way of life.

When they do learn to acknowledge their specific needs, to speak them, and to expect that they will be met, those with this as a primary structure can then thrive. They are in the role of "a people person" and are empathically aware of others' needs, making them very good in the service professions and compassionate as friends. Because they can be non-threatening and joyful, they can be very easy to trust, and thus allow others to readily find comfort and solace in relationship with them.

The disorders common to this style are diabetes, where the body does not make enough of its own insulin to fill its own needs, and low immune function (due to the lack of physical activity and stimulation), as well as addictions and obesity (bodily imaging their belief that they cannot get enough to be filled). Hoarding is also a byproduct of never getting enough. The perceived lack of sweetness in their life and their inability to be filled contributes to their physical difficulties.

CHAPTER EIGHT

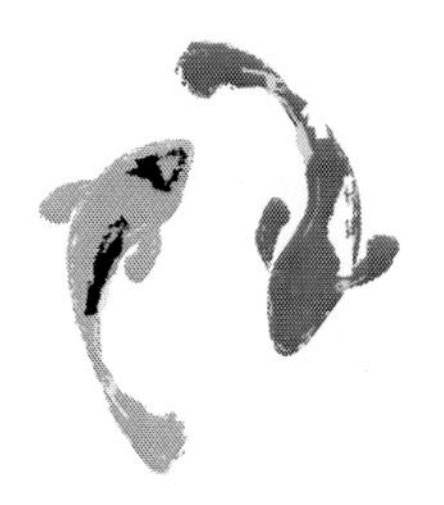

Nurturer/Masochist Structure

Nurturer/Masochist Overview

Healthy Characteristics

- Reliable
- Hard Working
- Persevering
- Loyal
- Nurturing
- Capable of great love.

Unhealthy Characteristics

- Afraid to take risks
- Passive-aggressive
- Views self as weak
- Strong-willed, endures long past time to stop
- Enmeshing – co-dependency
- Needs partner to define them.

Relationship Styles

- Very supportive
- Makes sacrifices easily
- Very affectionate and loving
- Passive-aggressive
- Will feel victimized and overwhelmed frequently
- Will transform self to fill partner's expectations and wants.

<u>Basic Beliefs</u>

- I am loved because of what I do, not who I am
- It is not OK to have fun
- I would if I could, but I can't
- I am powerless
- Strength comes from the will to keep pushing
- We all need to be loved and nurtured.

<u>Common Illnesses</u>

- Liver problems
- Chronic Fatigue
- Breast cancer
- Digestive disorders
- Exhaustion/dehydration
- Ulcers.

Nurturer/Masochist:

The wound of this structure develops around the time of conscious bowel movements and self-feeding. The message the children hear is that they will be loved if they follow their parents' demands, including body function schedules in terms of when and how much. If they are praised when they "performed" and penalized or humiliated when they didn't, the children learn that, to be loved and avoid humiliation, they need to know the expectations of the "other," and, thus, fill them.

They learn to embrace energetic repression and, finally, because they have no significance, to ignore their own needs and wants, since it is fulfilling the needs and wants of their parents that supports their being loved. The children come to believe they are loved because of what they do, not for who they are, and, therefore, as adults, they will overdo and over-commit, just to be loved sufficiently.

As adults, they frequently become involved in a large number of committees at their church or synagogue, to show their support. However, because of being over-extended, they are not able to fully commit their time or energy to any one committee or responsibility, thus leaving many things hanging or partially completed. Others may become legitimately angry at the lack of timely follow-through, which then puts the others in an awkward position. Rather than recognize s/he has dropped the ball, the masochist goes into victim or overwhelm (a familiar picture from childhood), feeling enraged at not being appreciated for what s/he did do. This is an easier reaction for such folks than acknowledging that perhaps they have over-extended themselves and need to let go of a number of their involvements.

As children, they got lost in the over-responsibility of a belief that they would be loved more because of what they did than because of who they are. In truth, if others love you, it is irrelevant how much you do or don't do. They love your energy; they love what you bring to every get-together, the insight perhaps, or the gentleness, the warmth, or the inspiration. These are the elements that are the highest qualities of your core essence. They reflect the true qualities of who you are, and have nothing to do with what service you do or do not perform for anyone.

When the Nurturer/Masochists are in an unhealthy state, enmeshment is the pattern of the relationships. As an example, because of their empathic nature, they will attune to another's moods and then have the same experience. It's because they are not self-defined, but instead defined by those with whom they are in relationship. They may literally ask who it is their partner wants them to be. In feeling their partner's feelings, in liking their partner's likes, they believe they are showing their total love for the other.

Rescuing the people they love becomes an obligation, whether those folks want to be rescued or not. For a Nurturer/Masochist, it is a sign of caring. If and when they can't rescue the stressed or wounded by making them feel better, the Nurturer/Masochist will become wounded, as well. They are thus joined together in the experience.

For people of this character structure, anxiety exists because of their need to make everyone happy, and they fear that they may not; it can become overwhelming. Rather than coming from a level of solid and grounded intent in what they do, helping to the extent that they can simply because those of this structure are naturally loving and kind people, they will come from a very strong will when they are in defense, with the ability to push far beyond the point where so many others would stop. They have an agenda to fix or to support, and they will endure until they reach that point, or collapse. Rarely do they go to bed when they are tired; they wait until they are exhausted.

For these individuals, self-betrayal occurs when their connection to their own essence gets lost as unimportant, since tending to the needs of others takes precedence. Because of their conditioned response to attune to and satisfy the needs of others, their focus stays outside of themselves. They have a propensity to become involved with controlling individuals who tell them what to do and when to do it. Although they may come to resent this dynamic, initially there is a joy at having someone else who so clearly can state what they want, need, and like. It appears on the surface that filling their partner's needs will be easy, love-filled, and highly rewarding.

However, as the anger builds over time, at the feeling of being invisible or unimportant other than in service, their anger comes out passive-aggressively. They are frightened and do not know how to utilize their power or their anger in honest self-expression. "I would if I could but I can't" is a common expression for these folks. They see themselves as weak, and yet they have a very strong will. When they are in defense, they do not risk confronting things directly, for fear they will lose any argument to their more powerful partner. As a result, they tend to act out in a less obvious way, aggressively and yet much more passively than expected.

An example of this strong will used in a passive-aggressive format involves a woman who came to see me after visiting doctors throughout the country for pains throughout her body that not one could clearly define. No one had been able to help her, so she was referred to my office. She had been a floor nurse for over 20 years, yet, due to this pain, she had gone to a part-time schedule. Eventually, she needed to quit working altogether, because the pain had been too much to bear. After a few minutes of talk therapy, I put her on my table for healing work.

There was an extensive amount of holding taking place so that her energy was highly coagulated, or dense, with minimal flow. She had a great amount of rage, hurt, and fear held throughout her body. Over her heart, I could sense a very hurt little girl who felt so alone. Because that area was so undefended, I was able to begin the healing and balancing process there and then move out to support the integration of this locally held experience into her whole body, bringing it all up to the level needed to match that of her healing heart chakra.

When she came back the following week, I asked how she felt, and she, in turn, told me that, after all these years, over 90% of the pain was gone. She asked if I could remove the last 10%. I told her that I would see what we could do together. She stood up and started to walk out of the room. When I asked why she was leaving, she told me quite emphatically that she would "not get rid of all the pain, because that bas----- was going to pay."

When I asked who that person was, she relayed that her husband had had an affair 10 years ago and that she was going to make sure that he would never spend another minute of his life without her at his side. If he went to the store, she needed to go along, since he never shopped correctly, even with a list. If he ran errands, she needed to get out of the house for some fresh air, so she went along.

If he got a haircut, she needed one also. Left with the possibility of being completely healed, she chose instead to suffer for the rest of her life, in order to make someone pay for an offense he had committed against her. For her, the price was worth it; yet, even when she won, she lost.

Another trait for this structure is that they can have a very difficult time justifying relaxing and having fun, since there is usually someone else in need. My mother, God bless her soul, was a natural in this structure. Years ago, when my children were small, they would give me their school notices as they were going to bed, or on their way out the door to school. Inevitably, I would make the brownies, or cupcakes, or write the checks needed for a school outing after signing the permission slips.

One May, I needed several hundred dollars immediately for my two children to sign up for summer camp. They had "forgotten" to give me the slip. I would not have the money available for another three weeks, but I called my mother, asking her if I could borrow $1,000 for three weeks. We had never been really close, and she often complained about my independence. I thought this would make her feel good, helping both myself and two of her grandchildren.

When I asked her, the response was silence, and then a long sigh. She then said, "Sure, Dan and I don't need to go on that vacation we have been saving all year for." I said, "Mom, when is that vacation?" She said "In November." I reminded her that I would pay her back in three weeks, in mid-June, long before her scheduled vacation. Her comment was, "No, Dan and I will just skip our vacation."

I felt that the only response I could offer without guilt was, "Never mind, Mom, the kids will just need to learn to tell me when they get these notices, and when I ask if they have any, tell me then." Another sigh...

This is when I knew I never should have asked, and then had to ask myself, where do I go from here? When I asked what was wrong, she said, "You never let me help you. I help all the others, and yet you never ask me for anything." My brothers and sister were much better at this than I was. The scenario I perceived was, if I take the money, she gives up her vacation, and we will all know that it was Dottie's fault; if I don't take the money, she is now hurt, because I never ask for anything.

My brothers and sister were going to love this one. I took the money. Mom's essence was that of a very powerful, loving, generous woman. Her ability to do martyrdom, however, made accepting that generosity an adventure that required great humor and resiliency.

The self-betrayal that exists within this structure is that such folks are intrinsically loving, nurturing, and kind, and yet, because they believe that the greater the suffering involved the greater they will be loved, they need to make every sacrifice that demonstrates how much they are willing to suffer. If an act of kindness and nurturance came from their soul's essence, they would simply enjoy the ability to help another, and suffering and sacrifice would not be an element of the act.

For the woman in the first example, loving would permit forgiveness, or moving on, rather than nurturing a wound to keep the pain alive and causing another to suffer endlessly. Getting caught in the emotions and the wound shows the defensive response, while coming from the intent to love, without cost, demonstrates the kindness of the soul.

Characters in entertainment who demonstrate this structure are Chandler from "Friends," Ray's mom on "Everybody loves Raymond," Hagrid in "Harry Potter," The Cowardly Lion in "Wizard of Oz," Rodney Dangerfield, and, finally, Ben Stiller's character in "Meet the Parents." Figures who reflect the healthy component of this include Florence Nightingale, Mother Theresa, and Nelson Mandela. Each of these powerful individuals were long-suffering in many ways, yet also very loyal to their cause, capable of great love, hard workers, and persevering—key qualities of the healthy manifestation of this structure and wonderful people to emulate.

When those whose primary structure is Nurturer/Masochist reach a point of claiming their own right to exist, to need, and to flourish, they can claim all the power they used in service to support their own unfolding. As powerful people, they are then immensely reliable, loyal, and hard working, with limits, and with a great capacity to love. They have no need for a leadership position, yet they will joyfully support a leader they believe in with their intelligence, hard work, and commitment. Their kindness makes them easy to love and to turn to when you need a friend. They are a gift to everyone in their life because of their innate joy, warmth, and ability to love unconditionally.

The physical propensities for disorder within this structure include chronic fatigue, which has a great deal to do with pushing one's self to follow a script that is not wanted, becoming tired of one's life, if you will; adrenal collapse, which can happen when every need of the other is an emergency that needs immediate attention; and breast cancer, which can be a consequence of nurturing the world, without permission to nurture the self. There can also be digestive disorders, liver disorders, and muscle spasms.

CHAPTER NINE

Leader/Psychopath Structure

Leader/Psychopath Overview

Healthy Characteristics

- Good leaders – managers
- Powerful speakers
- Charismatic
- Creative – generous
- Entertaining – charming
- Cool under fire.

Unhealthy Characteristics

- Control at all costs
- Intimidating
- Manipulative
- Narcissistic
- Demanding to be supported
- Rage.

Relationship Styles

- Adventurous
- Outgoing
- Protective
- Strong willed – forceful
- Limited ability for intimacy
- Must be center of relationship.

<u>Basic Beliefs</u>

- If I don't control you, you will control me
- We are all here to contribute in some way
- You can get close to me, as long as you look up to me
- I will never show my hurt to anyone
- I must be in control to be safe
- I don't need anyone.

<u>Common Illnesses</u>

- Stress related muscles spasms and disorders
- High blood pressure
- Gallbladder disorders
- Stroke
- Heart Attack
- Digestive disorders.

Leader/Psychopath

The wound of this structure usually presents around the age of three when the child is old enough to consciously begin to understand the concept of power even if there is no understanding of the dynamics behind it. As the child reaches the stage of seeking independence, perhaps in dressing themselves or picking out their own clothes, they are clearly saying that they want to have a say in their lives. They then begin to experiment with how far this illusion of independence and power can be expressed. For those with this as their primary structure, the child, male or female, was usually given a great deal more power in his or her family unit than what he or she was able to handle.

One example that supports unintentional wounding and confusion with the child could be shown as follows. Say that parents are planning to go out for the evening and their young son cries to mom for her to stay home, and speaks about how pretty she is, how much he likes her to read to him and tell him stories, and how he wants her to stay home and be with him and not go out with daddy,As a result, she cancels her plans.The first time that happens, the child gets excited that she stayed. He feels special and as a result he feels loved.

If it happens again, he begins developing a personality style in which he clearly knows how to become special and thus get his needs or wants met. Parents may even address him as their "special little boy" or "little man." How he achieves that specialness depends upon what works in that particular family system. If he takes a temper tantrum when his parents say they are going out, and mom says, "He is only young for a short while, let's stay home," this child has learned to control this family through rage. If it is done such as in the first example, the child has learned to be special through seduction. If the child works his will through manipulation such as telling mom that if she stays home he will go right to sleep and be happy all night, he has learned to be special and to control through manipulation.

The larger picture of all this is that the child has learned that at a young age he is actually in control of his parents and what they do and don't do. What an amazingly powerful position to be in! The bigger picture, however, also demonstrates that rather than having two parents who are guiding his life, this child has a mother who has become his ally, giving him far more power than he can handle and than he deserves, and a dad who has repeatedly felt put aside for the child.

As a result, subtly or otherwise, he is thus betrayed by mom, who stops being his strength and solid rock and who, instead, becomes his ally. Dad becomes his competition, as well as his safe haven. The dynamics in the home become cloudy and less defined. This child has found a power he did not know he had. With that can come a great deal of fear, since now, his safety is in his own hands. If he is the powerful one here, he can feel very vulnerable and at risk.

If the child was able to get his demands met through seduction, then that is the style he will use in adulthood with his wife, friends, and others. He knows it works. If his demands were met through manipulation, he has learned to manipulate in all his relationships. If intimidation or anger worked for him, he will take that one strategy into his adult life as a means of getting his way and to get his needs and wants met. His defense structure, developed to keep him safe and special, becomes his way of life as an adult. As a spouse, co-worker, parent, or employee, his style or tools for getting his needs met are established and will be used. However, if one (such as seduction), does not work, he can apply any or all of the other approaches. The bottom line is getting his needs met and feeling safe being in control.

Energetically, this style projects a great deal of strength, and, depending upon their presentation, such adults may quickly take control of a room or a situation, naturally. Their belief, in defense, is that they must be in control or someone will hurt or destroy them. Consequently, to get the support and encouragement they need, they will attempt to control in any way they can through seduction, manipulation, or intimidation. In a clear way, they will let it be known that their relationships revolve around their needs and wants. It is their charm and seduction, that make others want to give them the control. If that doesn't work, then manipulation or intimation ensures that happening.

In relationship, as well, when they are in defense, they need to be the "special" one of the couple whether that is smarter, more powerful, or so on. This prevents the ability for mutual intimacy that we all crave since true mutual intimacy can only exist between equals where the uniqueness in each is valued rather than the specialness of just one.

Actors such as Matthew McConaughey, Tom Selleck, George Clooney, Al Pacino, and Charles Bronson, and characters such as Joey Tribbiani from "Friends" and Sam Malone in "Cheers," often portray the defensive component of this character structure, as does Angelina Jolie as Lara Croft, Evelyn Harper as the mom on "Two and a Half Men," and Glen Close as Alex Forrest in "Fatal Attraction." Healthy leadership models of this structure include Martin Luther King and John F. Kennedy, both men who could call many to follow their lead simply because of who they were and what they stood for.

When they come from their essence, those with this structure are naturally gifted leaders who know how to train and develop those they work with. They support others in claiming their strengths, as well as in working for the good of the team. They can be very powerful and charismatic speakers, motivators, and leaders with a great gift for entertaining others while simultaneously being wonderfully calm and supportive in crises. Because they tend to be outgoing and adventurous, they can be a lot of fun and desired company. They bring a significant amount of charm and creativity to their work and play when they are balanced, and are a joy to have in a group since others may readily follow them.

The gift they bring is a willingness and skill in leadership that makes others want to support or help participate in any program. The strength and willingness to be seen, and honored, calls them to take charge when a leader is needed, and, being intelligent, they tend to have many alternative options available when one is needed to support progress and make things happen.

We certainly need leaders at this point in our history. It appears that there are many who want to fight for their position politically, but they are doing so in hysteria, part of the schizoid structure, in extreme neediness, the oral structure, or as overwhelmed victims and blamers, the masochistic structure. What we need, however, is someone who can lead because of his ability to see what needs to be done, and who can present it in such a way as to get masses following. Obviously, it requires one who has the ability to adjust his style as needed to achieve the highest of results and who can get others to follow his lead, however he gets there.

In their truth, these leaders are confident and comfortable in their own skin. They learn from their employees while calling each to speak his or her mind, develop the skills to lead, and very willingly delegate to others to share the glory and the responsibility of the task. As a leader in my office, I wanted every person at the meeting to present his or her thoughts on the latest project. They each possessed skills I did not, and to hear what each thought allowed me to expand my vision and to see options I never would have thought of on my own. It also supported them in recognizing the gifts they brought to the table, thus making them a stronger team member. Confidence can do that and see that reality – removing the idea of threats and control from the table.

The physical disorders I have seen to be most common with this style of personality are high blood pressure, high cholesterol, gallstones, and heart attacks. Those who rule from will need to stay vigilant and fight to win the "kill." The price their body pays is high.

CHAPTER TEN

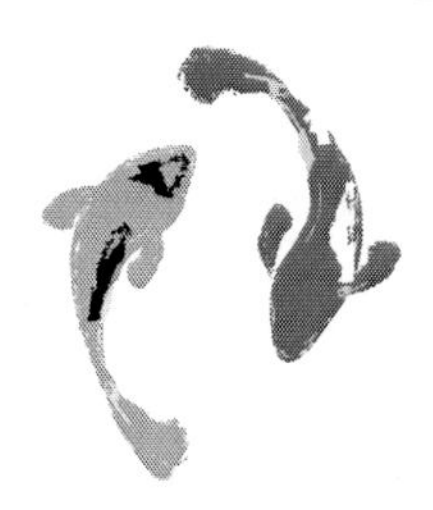

Achiever/Rigid Structure

Achiever/Rigid Overview

Healthy Characteristics

- High achievers – successful
- Fastidious workers
- Self-confident
- Organized
- Responsible
- Predictable.

Unhealthy Characteristics

- Tries to gain approval through perfection
- Disconnected from emotions
- Over-achievers
- Must be right at all times
- Heart – Sex disconnect
- Righteous superiority.

Relationship Styles

- Maintains healthy boundaries
- Capable of great love
- Open to growth
- Competitive
- Holds back
- Has all the right answers.

Basic Beliefs

- If I cannot do it perfectly, I will not do it at all
- I have to achieve with significance to be OK
- It is far more important to be perfect and appropriate than to be real
- If I don't love you, you can't hurt me
- I will find the one, perfect way to do things
- My world must be in perfect order.

Common Illnesses

- Heart disease
- Lungs
- Thymus
- Asthma
- Circulation
- Obsessive-compulsive disorder.

Achiever/Rigid

Those with this last structure have as their greatest wound the feeling of not being good enough, even to themselves. Because who they were was irrelevant, they have lost sight of their core essence and essentially what makes them who they are. While growing up, they got a clear message that who they were wasn't anywhere near as important as how they projected, or looked to others. Where they ranked competitively was also what counted. Consequently, the need to be perfect and appropriate at all times in order to be valued and respected governs their behavior, as well as their experience and judgment of themselves. This individual has learned that being real is not important, and probably not appropriate.

Although this structure can begin as early as three years of age, it is solidified around the time of puberty. If you have ever lived with a teenager, you will understand the context. As with most adolescents, when these children arrive home from school, they may love the world. By the time they get into the kitchen, they hate life. Once they go to their room, they may feel that they have no friends. Once the phone rings, they feel very popular again and thus very happy. For some of us, this is a reason simply to thank God we are not teenagers any more—and to thank God we do not have teenagers at home any more, even though, when we did have teenagers going through puberty in the house, it was a time of compassion, confusion, and laughter—and great love. That stage of parenting, for some, was certainly an adventure we shared daily with our friends and family concerning mood swings, emotions, friendships, boyfriends or girlfriends, and so much else. We all survived it together, in the sharing.

However, for those parents who believe that there is a place for everything and a thing for every place, having this lack of order is threatening and disheartening. For some parents, emotions, especially those that are exaggerated around the time of puberty, are a sign of immaturity or a lack of sophistication. They are uncomfortable, usually because of their own upbringing, with the wide variance, unpredictability, and intensity of teenage emotionality.

The adolescent children of such parents quickly get the message that both emotions and sexuality are inappropriate. Thus, these kids learn to disconnect from their emotions and from their sexuality. These factors are connected so closely because it is in puberty, while having their first conscious wave of sexual feelings, that their emotions are also running free reign and the opposite sex stops being gross. When their behavior is considered inappropriate at this point, it is too hard to distinguish between the aspects which are being judged, so simply rejecting it all is the safest bet.

In order to gain their parents' acceptance and to make their parents comfortable, and as an added demonstration of their perfection or appropriateness, these adolescents demanded high success from themselves in all areas. They tend as teens to be very competitive and the best in whatever they do, with no tolerance for second place.

If they actually find themselves in second place, they see themselves as failures. The love they receive from their parents feels conditional, and, as a result, they need to achieve and produce beyond normal limits. The lack of emotional acceptance or the expression of that acceptance in their home prevents them from reaching out in an emotional way to be loved and approved of.

The struggle to be who they "should" be while recognizing, as well, that something is missing can support a downward spiral into depression. The something that is missing in their lives is themselves. In their pursuit of appropriateness and perfection as defined by others, they have lost touch with the essence of their own soul, as well as with the gentleness of their heart. It can be very difficult to believe they are truly loved, since they do not see their intrinsic worth or goodness, only their failings and limitations, making it difficult to have a truly intimate relationship as an adult.

Everything is measured as to what it should be or who they should be. They learned to listen to the outside, rather than listening to the inner conversation that would have reminded them of who they were and why they were here. The inner voices eventually were ignored since they had no relevance to life as they lived it.

I have had many adults come into my office who, when I ask how they feel, would say something to the effect of, "I have no idea how I feel. I have been putting my right foot in front of my left for most of my life. I don't know what I feel about anything."

Ultimately, their disconnection from their emotions and their sexuality results in a separation between the heart and their genitals. It is not uncommon to see that a healthy and active sex life before marriage for these folks changes dramatically after marriage. If they permit themselves, they will come into an office similar to mine to find out what happened. The fear of giving someone both their heart and their sexuality is terror causing - an investment and an exposure that is beyond intimidating. Investing their self-image to such an extent that so much of who they are would be exposed and could be rejected is far too threatening. It is not uncommon to see, after marriage, that their spouse and family is provided with this person's heart and relationship commitment, while it is their lover who gets to experience that same person's joy, emotions, and uninhibited sexuality. The sex/heart split makes it possible; the need to be seen as perfect makes it mandatory.

When those who have this as a primary structure are in defense, they can look and feel very brittle, very tight. They are holding themselves in an appropriate manner, rather than in a relaxed and informal fashion, even in an informal setting. Much of their posture is due to the fact that they tend to carry much of their energy in their back, or will, areas. As a result, they are rigidly held, and move without grace or fluidity. Physically, and in their presentation, they look perfect with every hair in place and their clothes in perfect condition, even their leisure wear.

In contrast, when they are healthy and not in defense, they can feel very vibrant, motivated, and alive. Because they have high energy and are powerful as well as achievers, they are capable of easily planning and organizing any event that interests them. Working on a task force with them is rewarding because things move smoothly and expeditiously, making it an enjoyable task where you can readily feel the accomplishment coming together. In this healthy state, they are fun to be with and a joy to work with.

At this point they are also able to form deep personal relationships, because they have connected with their emotions and their desire to be in relationship. Professionally, as adults, they readily enter positions such as that of engineer, accountant, and banker. These fields that demand perfection and make it attainable satisfy them, at least for a while. Because they are analytical, they can be very resourceful when that is needed in dealing with a problem.

Some of the well known examples of this structure are Monica from "Friends," Felix Unger from the "Odd Couple," the Tin Man from "The Wizard of Oz," Will from "Will and Grace," and Hermione from "Harry Potter." The healthy examples of this structure include all those who are able to sustain a safe place while dealing with so many of the day-to-day challenges that are presented, with love, warmth, and order.

Although these several structures appear to be unrelated, the reality is that every individual has some of each. The proportion in which you have them defines your unique personality, including your approach to life and to relationships. The proportions also help to define who will be attractive to you. Your attractions, on an unhealthy level, support you in repeating behaviors related to the unresolved issues from your past. In a healthy state, your attractions support you in being with the people from whom you can learn to develop those traits you most seek in yourself as well as resolve past issues completely.

Traditionally, someone who is primarily Oral will be partnered with someone who is more Rigid and self-sufficient. The Oral structure can rely on the more Rigid individual to be able to make things happen as needed. Those who are primarily Rigid are able to do what needs to be done and to get it done well. The Rigid personality, in being with someone who is primarily Oral, gets to be with someone who, when healthy, can clearly express his or her own needs, and who, hopefully, knows how to get them met.

The Masochist, who is fighting to be free from oppression or being told what to do, will become involved with someone with a strong Psychopathic structure who has the need to control. It gives the Masochists the chance to fight for their freedom and their right to claim their own power. The other structures either would not engage in battle or would readily give in, thus eliminating the satisfaction of winning for the masochist. Those with a Psychopathic primary structure find someone who is willing to let them define their partner and who will loyally and patiently support them in their every want and desire, allowing them to be the center of this relationship.

Whatever the unhealthy reasons for a match, once each or both of those in the relationship choose to grow, choose to come alive and live in relationship to themselves, listening to their own body/soul conversation, the dynamics will change. As each of you remembers who you truly are, you have far greater access to your essence and an easy path back to your truth. By choosing to live in essence, and not from the level of personality, you choose to step into the deeper, more fulfilling, and more peaceful aspects of your journey.

You also come from your own heart/soul connection, making it so much easier to be empathic and understanding with those you love. Your relationships then change and the ability to come from the highest qualities of your personality, of your character structures, increases significantly. From this mind-set, you are able to look at your fears, your wounds, and your beliefs and put them in perspective. Whether they come from your past or your present, you are not your personality, you are so much more. Remembering that opens you up to going deeper into the reality of who you are now, exploring the level of wound as needed, while focusing on the gift of feeling alive in ways you never imagined.

Think of how your energy feels in those moments when everything in your life seems fine and you know that you are not connected to any fear or self-hatred at that moment. Now recall how it feels when you are consumed with fear and the resultant rage or illusionary victimization, and the subsequent collapse. If you can bring both those experiences into your physical consciousness at this moment, you will be able to see how quickly your body can shift its energy pattern and what a difference it makes in your body, your outlook, and your life.

All this is within your control at any moment in time, if you only choose to live in conscious awareness of your personality (your persona), your fears, and your journey inward. That consciousness, that quietness, and that peaceful awareness makes listening to your body/soul connection a natural process and one that will change your life—while giving you, "you."

CHAPTER ELEVEN

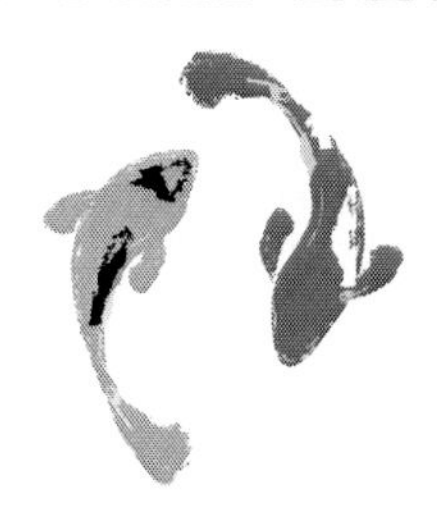

Our Wounds

All of your defensive reactions which are lived through the character structures we have just discussed are held onto as a result of your past wounds and your beliefs around them. If as a child you were consistently humiliated if you did not know something, unless you recognize that it was the result of another's self-hatred and had nothing to do with you, you will go through life believing that you know little and expecting to be humiliated for it. If as a child you were slapped or beaten each time you made a mistake, you will go into adulthood believing you are dumb and expecting others to hurt you because of it. In my experience as a psychotherapist, I have found that, as an adult, you tend to bring someone into your life who will repeat the expected behavior in their relationship with you. Because experience has taught you that such treatment is normal in relationships, you will tolerate that treatment far longer than someone who has never been treated in that way.

Every time someone has a different opinion than yours, you will withhold yours for fear you could be punished or negated. You may become frightened of expressing an opinion, even if it is similar, for fear you will say it wrong and could be in trouble as a result. Consequently, you will either be waiting for someone to put you down or you will be too frightened to have anything to say. In response to the wound and your very deep need to feel safe and loved, you develop an energy pattern to protect yourself. This guarding against the wound or emotion becomes the defense structure.

When you are overly aware of a wound, you believe you cannot heal; you focus outside of yourself on everyone else and what s/he said or did against you. As a response, you may become filled with rage and readily express it at any perceived affront to your ego. Everyone you meet will be a potential challenge causing you to live your life in a rage-fueled defense to protect against further wounding. The opposite reaction could be that you perceive all others as having the ability to negate you and that there is nothing you can do to prevent that from occurring except to try constantly to be good enough in order to avoid the abuse.

In either case, you begin to disappear within your own life. Your focus leaves your inner journey, your body/soul connection, and your attention remains external in anticipation of the next uncomfortable or negating experience. It becomes a conditioned response, a reaction to your past with little recognition that you have the ability to make your present different. You live in the past and continue to replay it, recreating those situations again and again. When you are alone, you can even trigger your defense through the mental messages you repeat to yourself: "I'm not good enough," "I'm stupid." "I'm all alone."

As you can see in the figure on the next page, it is the conscious decision for personal growth and the choice to live mindfully that permits you to take a new approach to your everyday way of life while bringing in far more joy and power than you are accustomed to.

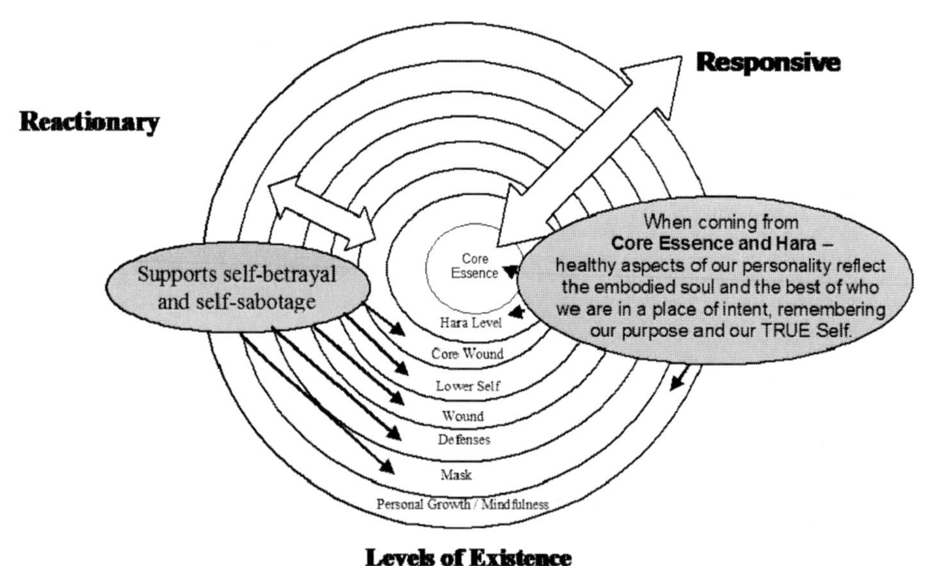

Levels of Existence
Figure 1 – Reactionary VS Responsive

In reviewing what we have already discussed, by looking at what masks you wear, you begin to understand the way in which you avoid owning your own truth. Once you can accept, without judgment, what masks you have used in order to support yourself feeling loved or safe, you can then look at what it is that pulls you to hold onto the masks so strongly so that you let them go, or conversely, go further into defensive reaction rather than a chosen healthy response. To go a step further, acknowledging when you go into defensive reaction supports you further in achieving awareness of what particular behavior from others you have been protecting yourself against.

It is too late to protect yourself from the old wounds; they already exist. You may deny them, but they are there, hurting you again and again. The concept behind the saying that those who fear death die a thousand times applies here. Those who live in fear of their past wounds are preventing them from being healed and thus suffer from those wounds again and again, all the while fearing they will continue to be wounded in relationship again and again.

Sadly, because the wounds occurred when we were children, they were, and are, perceived through the eyes of a child. Children can often see things as being far greater or far smaller than they really are and take that perception with them into adulthood. An example of this took place with my family. Years ago, when my children were 10 and 6, and we were living in a wealthy suburb, I took them to see the housing projects where I grew up.

I had told them the front doors to the building were far larger than normal. I had also told them that as a first-grader my boyfriend and I had carved our initials in very large letters into the inside of the front door, taking hours to do so. When we arrived at my old building, I was shocked to find that the door was standard height. The very large letters were probably one to two inches tall. I was shocked. My memory had such clear, and yet very different, pictures.

Of course, now I can see they were the pictures taken with the eyes of a 7 year old. Lying on that floor, carving our initials in that door, probably did take hours with whatever little knife we had. Needing to pretend we were just sitting there each time someone came in must have made the process a whole lot slower than it would otherwise have been.

That experience with my children allowed me to see how powerful perception is. It also caused me to rethink so many things about my childhood. There had been many things I needed to minimize to survive the journey, and things I needed to block from my memory to feel safe and loved, as if I belonged. These skills in avoidance helped me to see my childhood as I needed it to be and supported me in becoming who I am. Being able to look at and deal with situations later, when I had greater skills and understanding, also supported me in moving forward and consciously defining how I would live my adult life and what world views I wanted to hold as an adult.

As a child, if you were abused by one or more adults, you could come to see the world itself as being abusive. If you were negated, you come to believe that no one wants you. You come to see events and people through the lens of the child, and you come to embody the defenses that allowed that child to survive. That reaction may have helped the child to survive physically or to stay sane emotionally, yet when you become an adult, those same reactions, those beliefs, and those defenses can serve as tools for betrayal and self-inflicted wounding.

These responsive energy patterns, these defenses, may no longer be needed, but if they aren't even recognized, they are lived with as if they are a part of you. Over time, you can forget who you are without the defenses because you have lived with them most of your life. Where does who you are begin, and where do the defenses begin and end?

For example, if you see yourself as unwanted, then each time someone forgets to call you or walks by without saying hello, your lens, your filter, tells you it is because they do not like you or want you around. You are convinced this is the truth. Because of such a strong bias, you cannot believe, even if you are told, that what actually happened was that they had a sick child rushed to the hospital and forgot everything, or perhaps that their mind was on an impending meeting they were anxious about and they walked right by you without seeing you.

Regardless, you will believe that if they really wanted to speak to you, they would have at least called, no matter what the circumstance, even briefly, or said hello. You will always be the victim and unwanted because your lens perceives all events through that filter. What once protected you and kept you safe from abuse now prevents you from claiming your place in your life and from honoring those who are walking with you in trusting what they say, and in seeing them as good, caring folks who care even though they are human.

If there is something you don't like about yourself, and we all seem to have something – or many things – look at what it is. Is it truly who you are or is it a behavior pattern from your past? Does it reflect the truth of who you want to be or is it a reactionary pattern you never realized you had? Learning to fully experience your body, to know what it is feeling and why, permits you to be more open and accepting, less judgmental, and more loving with yourself and, eventually, with others. In recognizing that a certain perception, a certain bias, or a certain defensive reaction is simply old material, you have the option of choosing to do it differently.

You must first recognize, or own your options, as well as your tendencies, if effective and long-standing change is to take place. Assessing your filter, and checking it with someone you trust, allows you to understand when your filter is up, limiting your ability to see things clearly. Checking in with another when needed can prevent unnecessary and harmful hurt from impacting your day and your relationships.

As a licensed marriage and family therapist, I have seen many relationships destroyed because at least one partner is not in relationship with his or her actual partner, but, instead, with his or her perception of who the other is. Who s/he is seeing and resenting is actually a parent or previous partner, yet, because of the filter s/he is wearing, the new person's actions and words are tainted with old expectations that may have nothing to do with who the new person actually is.

This is a perfect example of repeating old wounds as well as betraying yourself and those with whom you are in relationship. It is unnecessary and yet, sadly, not uncommon. Thankfully, it is all workable, if you are willing to grow.

Your Core Wound, which is basically the origin of the particular wounds you recreate along this journey, is a wound that permeates all of your life and all your belief systems. If your Core Wound is that you are not good enough, you will not be good enough as an employee or good enough as a partner, a mother, a daughter or son, or even a friend. The consistency of the theme in your life, however, allows you to more readily identify it when you are ready to do so.

If your Core Wound is that you do not belong, you will feel that you do not belong anywhere, at least when looking through your filter. If you are invited to lunch by your office mates, you will believe they did it out of pity or obligation. If your in-laws treat you well and ask about you, you will believe it is their effort to be nice that prompted those behaviors, since you will not believe that you really are welcomed and/or wanted. It is difficult to feel at home with them, or, really, with anyone.

Because the Core Wound is so deep and is such a governing force in your filter, it is believed by some that such wounds are possibly an aspect of your personality that you have brought with you from a previous lifetime to be healed.

CHAPTER TWELVE

Lower Self

This journey inward, to your own essence, to the truth of who you are as an embodied soul, may appear long at this point, but it needn't be. I am presenting it in a linear format so that you can see the process, yet, thankfully, we are not linear people and can bounce along going back and forth between these stages. (How unfortunate for those folks who try hard to have it be linear, since the natural approach can be unpredictable and requires that you use your creativity and spontaneity frequently.)

The truth is, you can have moments when it feels as if you are dying because of the pain, and then, "out of nowhere," comes a moment when you experience yourself, or life, as the clear, pure, unlimited, awesome reality that it is. Those are the moments that give you the strength to keep going when needed. For me, they are also the moments when I see that there is something so much greater than I am out there somewhere, and in here somewhere.

Those moments, for me, help it all make sense. In that split second, I realize that life is so much bigger than I am and that I am so much bigger than the crisis I have created at the moment. AHA moments make it seem so obvious that what we think and feel is a choice, because, if we notice, in a split second we can see, feel, and know that where we are at the moment is so changeable. It is a moment of putting life itself in perspective—and in a perspective that is freeing beyond words! It is at these times that I feel thoroughly thrilled that I am alive.

I am certain that a part of the reason for the joy is that, in those moments, I truly know, at the core of my being, that we have never walked alone on this planet. Not so amazingly, I have carried a prayer, some call it a poem, in my purse for over 30 years. It is now well-worn and torn in places, yet I know it well, since it has gotten me through some very difficult times. You may know it, as well, but what a wonderful thing to read again and again.

Footprints

One night a man had a dream. He dreamed
he was walking along the beach with the LORD.
Across the sky flashed scenes from his life.
For each scene he noticed two sets of
footprints in the sand: one belonging
to him, and the other to the LORD.
When the last scene of his life flashed before him,
he looked back at the footprints in the sand.
He noticed that many times along the path of
his life there was only one set of footprints.
He also noticed that it happened at the very
lowest and saddest times in his life.
This really bothered him and he
questioned the LORD about it:
"LORD, you said that once I decided to follow
you, you'd walk with me all the way.
But I have noticed that during the most
troublesome times in my life,
there is only one set of footprints.
I don't understand why when
I needed you most you would leave me."
The LORD replied:
"My son, my precious child,
I love you and I would never leave you.
During your times of trial and suffering,
when you see only one set of footprints,
it was then that I carried you."

Several different names are given as the author, including Unknown. The first version is thought to have been written by Mary Stevenson in 1936, although this version is attributed to Carolyn Carty from 1963. Reading this poem, for me, provides one of those moments when I can surrender, come apart from defense, and feel at peace with my life and my journey. Whatever it is that supports you in achieving that surrender, I wish that for you. I wish as well the ability to go there as often as you feel it is needed.

When I was growing up as an Irish Catholic girl in South Boston, MA, we heard about good angels leading you to God and bad angels leading you to the devil. Of course, we were warned to follow only the good angels; yet, I must confess that, at times, taking a risk and following the bad angel was fun. (It usually resulted in detention if it took place in school or in being punished or grounded if it took place after school.) At times, however, the price was worth it. Now we speak of spirits, guides, and angels. It seems to me that this is all the same reality, only the names have changed. In all of this, there is a message that says you have never walked alone. Whether you want to call your travel companions God, angels, spirits, or anything else that fits your faith system, you are not walking alone is the basic premise of the statement.

On occasion, when you do feel alone and threatened, however, there are times when, rather than going into one of the character structure's defensive components, as described earlier, you may come from a place known as the "Lower Self." Some theorists call it the "shadow-side," others the "dark-side." The different names for it have essentially the same meaning. It is that part of yourself—a reactionary aspect of your personality—that supports self-betrayal, destructiveness, greed, and distortion. It tends to show up when you are reacting to a wound, and yet, rather than feeling powerless in this place, you feel powerful. Rather than feeling emotionally reactive, it can feel very logical, thought out, and appropriate, at least for that part of you in that moment. You know that split second when you get an urge to pull the chair out of the way when someone is about to sit down, or when you want to spill something on someone's new outfit, or toy with the idea of giving someone the wrong directions? That's the moment when the Lower Self raises itself to consciousness.

It feels powerful, justified, and logical, based on your perspective at the moment. If you have ever followed that urge, you know how powerful and vindictive that feels at the moment. "Anyone else would have felt the same way or done the same thing" seems like the right assessment. However, a few minutes later, when you leave that energetic place, you realize you have just betrayed the truth of who you really are and who you really want to be—but it is too late, you did it... It was destructive, vindictive, and hurtful, and yet it felt so right for that split second. If you are honest, acknowledge the experience to yourself. Acknowledge as well the power and joy that comes with it.

In our humanity, it can be very easy to get the urge to do something along these lines. Eventually, perhaps, you may outgrow the desire, experience it only in extremely rare moments, and, even at those times, never consider actually acting upon it—only, hopefully, accept that you felt it. (Remember that whatever we deny, we hold in our body in a form similar to an energetic cyst. It needs to be acknowledged, and then allowed to flow through you, leaving you perhaps feeling grateful that you didn't act on it.) This acknowledgement supports your energy in freely flowing throughout your body, supporting your health on all levels. Acknowledging that aspect of yourself, recognizing that it exists in all of us, supports you in remaining humble, if you should ever reach the temporary illusion of being "done" with your personal development. As an aside, if you have a great sense of humor, you may find that you can laugh at yourself as well, amazed at your own ingenuity—but only if didn't do it, whatever "it" is!

As with everything, there is a good side to this element of your being, as well. When you harness the energy that exists in this aspect of yourself, the lower self, you have a very powerful, potent, and creative energy source that you can, in turn, use productively. Energy is neither good nor bad; it is only energy. How you use it defines it; so you simply need to redirect your intent and use it productively to support yourself or others. The Lower Self is governed by negative intent arising from the desire for negative pleasure, or pleasure from someone else's pain. Changing the intent to a positive allows all that power, all that creative capability, and all that passion to be used productively in supporting another or in moving forward in your own life. It is all great energy, flowing freely, and, with a good intent motivating it, you are transformed who it is you want to be and who you are in your essence.

If you remember, the defensive component of the character structures was developed in childhood to support you in either feeling loved by others or safe. The defenses were thought to be a means of keeping you connected—at whatever cost, and in whatever way possible. They are often a well-recognized aspect of your personality. The Lower Self aspect of your personality was also developed in childhood as a result of your wounds, yet, rather than going to a place of emotional fear and vulnerability, this aspect of your personality comes about while you are feeling powerful, creative, and vindictive.

Some children, after a painful experience, numb themselves to their wants and pain, and, in doing so, they simultaneously desensitize themselves to the wants and pain of others, making it easier to be self-centered and egocentric. Part of your personal growth process is the acknowledging of this aspect of yourself and bringing it into consciousness so you can see it and work with it. Rather than this aspect of self being the pink elephant in the room, by contrast, knowing where the Lower Self is, what it feels like to be in it, and how to transform it permits you to claim all the aspects of you, embody them, and celebrate the fullness of all the energy at your disposal. It is only energy, not good or bad, just energy. What you do with it, the intent you act on, defines how you use it, constructively or destructively.

CHAPTER THIRTEEN

Hara - Level of Intent

With the many levels of consciousness, and the many different wounds and gifts you possess, as you may have seen in the previous chapter, it is still primarily your intent, or lack of it, that defines the style and quality of the life you have. Dreams and visions are what make it possible for you to have a goal, and motivation, as you go through your day-to-day life. Without the ability to lock into intent, however, your dreams remain conversation starters and part of your Wish List. With intent, however, if you can dream it, and visualize it, you can make it happen. It is just about being willing to pay the price.

The greatest price is usually the commitment, passion, and desire required to achieve those dreams. These qualities are not easy to sustain without having a clear ability to hold yourself within the level of intent. Using your Will (a defensive reaction) can exhaust you and result in resentment and bitterness at the work entailed. Coming from the strength and peace of intent (response), however, permits you to take a break if it is needed and come back energized, feeling powerful and focused, rather than victimized.

I would like to make an observation that for those who truly want to be happy (which is quite different from constantly seeking out "fun"), it requires an attitude of adventure and detachment, permitting you to enjoy the gift and adventure of the trip and not just the escape of the moment. If it is your intent to pursue personal growth, to live mindfully, and to become aware of all the ways in which you go into defense, you can actually live a journey that becomes a life-long adventure of self-discovery, learning to love and accept yourself and others, along with the achieving of the joy in continued expansion. Being just who you are today, can get awfully boring, even for you.

Overall, it is a fun trip if you let it be. Take a break from growing when you need to. Allow yourself to numb out – through television, the movies, a vacation exploring new places or new people - whatever lets you take a break from your life. It makes coming home exciting again while making you grateful for all that you have brought into your life. In the process, you get to be far more objective.

Whether in seeing your limitations, failing at a particular goal, or missing something that was important to you, it all becomes simply a life lesson to learn from, not an excuse to give up, get angry, or go into self-hatred. Your intent to grow and become all that you are here to become, supports the reactionary mode, if it should occur, to be short-lived and simply accepted for what it is, another challenge that can strengthen your resolve to live in the truth of who you are, while accepting your humanity, with all its strengths and vulnerabilities, without judgment.

Give yourself a break. This isn't a contest or even a test; it's life. It is meant to be joyful not miserable; it is meant to flow not be arduous; and it is meant to be an exciting adventure not work. If it is difficult, what are you doing wrong? We all have hard times, we all have pain, and we all have losses. What we do with them defines us and the type of journey we are creating. They can't be escaped, but they are not meant to trap us either.

Think of folks you know who say, "I want to lose weight," or "I am going back to the gym," and never do either. That is because the comment comes from the personality level, not the level of intent. They may want to do those things because "they should," not because it is a part of who they are right now. Those are burdens and expectations they have placed on themselves that they do not truly want at this moment. As a result, to reach down deep within themselves to make it happen may be more than they are willing or able to do at the moment.

Their good intentions may come from fear, manipulation, or a momentary openness of their heart. When intentions do not come from the Hara, the level of intent, the cycle of stop and start—or perhaps the dead-end approach of never even getting started—begins. This is certainly the sad story of so many who want to lose weight or stop smoking. Thankfully, we all know someone who actually said they were going to stop and then did it. When you ask how, and why now, they will tell you, "It was just time." What that says to me is that all of who they are, on every level, was ready and their intent was set in motion.

True intent comes from a connection to your soul's longings and finding a place in your life for you and your current dream. When a statement is made from the conscious level of intent, it is already actualized in your body and in your mind. Now you just need to make it happen in the physical world, and you will do so without ambivalence or the common push/pull difficulties. This energy feels so different in your body. It feels solid, clarified, focused, and present—in other words, really good.

A common area of confusion in regard to intent is in the difference between intent and will. There can appear to be only a fine line of distinction, yet the gap between the two states is actually quite large. Living in intent allows you to keep your heart open, your energy flowing in balance, and yourself grounded, without defense or reaction. This is possible because, in intent, there is integration among all the aspects of who you are. When others meet you, they feel your solidity, your sense of self, and your purpose in this world.

In contrast, when you come from your will, there is a physical and energetic awareness of force within and around you. Others get a sense that you have experience pushing your way through a situation and that you will get to where you are going regardless of what it takes or, perhaps, who is in the way, even them.

Most definitely, intent and will feel very different both in the individual making the choice between them and as well as to those around them. The first comes from your center, the clear actualizing truth of who you are; the other comes from defense, as if fighting an enemy, whether that is an individual, an organization, or a project.

For those who have seen the seasoned Tai Chi and Qigong masters, it is clear they have an ability to focus in intent that is extraordinary.

Rather than such focus making their world smaller, it makes it larger, or more expansive. They have a full awareness of their inner world and the use of their energy, while also having a sense of the world around them that surpasses the norm. Watching the demonstration of a master who, through intent, has the ability to move a car or a large person from a distance, solely through intent and the ability to focus energy in a particular way, demonstrates the power of intent and the ability we can all achieve to impact our environment. Consequently, the illusion that we are powerless beings is shown to be a totally inaccurate statement. You all have the potential to attain this effective presence, but to do so, you need to be able, and willing, to step out of all reactionary thought, feeling, and behavior at that moment and into response in order to be present to different realities simultaneously. The ability to quiet the mind and to open the chakras so that all of your energy flows, is a goal of those who work toward this level of balance, presence, and true power.

Imagine your life if you were able to live in this state of consciousness as a way of being, rather than as a goal to achieve. I have had clients who were teachers of this work, yet they were still working on their ability to connect to their essence. For them, their life journey has been to take each step, as needed, to reach a place of conscious spiritual awakening. This step of living in and balancing their Hara is a conscious step for them in their progression of spiritual awakening and strengthening.

For others without a spiritual awareness or a desire to understand the bigger picture, yet who may want this level of intent, their effort is solely about the ability to succeed at something specific. I have heard some people called "single minded." Their ability to stay focused on their goal, whether it is success in business, in a sport, or in a personal accomplishment, is similar to that of the masters described above, although the objective is more immediate and limited. It is action-specific, rather than focused on establishing a spiritual way of life. Instead of becoming more expansive, their world becomes smaller with an ability to focus only on the one thing they crave rather than the world around them. Their life style causes them to lose touch with anyone and anything not in their line of focus.

The Hara itself is literally an energetic line, a spiritual center that passes through the crown of your head, through your body, straight down into the earth. It encompasses the Yin/Yang, the Female/Male energies of the earth and sky as they pass through you, reinforcing your connection to the spiritual and the worldly, to the feminine and the masculine energies of this planet and of you. In pictures of the Buddhist monks in meditation, you see them sitting with their fingers against their abdominal area. Within that area is considered to be the Tan Tien, a significant point along the Hara line, and the seat of universal wisdom.

Our intent, as a people, needs to honor this awareness of universal wisdom and the universality of all of us, human and non-human alike, so that we can each work to support and save the other. If a Martial Arts Master has the ability to move an object at a distance from himself through intent, and a mother, told she is dying, chooses not to die—regardless of a doctor's prognosis—because she believes her children need her, imagine the power of intent if, as a people, if we all chose to walk this earth as one family.

As we grow and learn, we need to see that what impacts one person or one country, impacts the others. I do not believe in accidents or coincidences. Could it be that global warming, the Tsunami, Hurricane Katrina, the cyclone in Burma, and the earthquake in China, Haiti, and Chile, all support further development of the realization that we all need each other and that we are all in this together, with an obligation to one another? If it were our intent as a people, the intent of many individuals on this planet, to eradicate hunger, to solve the problem of water shortage, I believe fully that it could be done.

The power of intent is immense. The power that comes when many people are joined in intent magnifies itself. We simply need to learn to live from that place within ourselves and support self-care and the care of others. If it is our intent as a people, it will be done. Force is not always the solution; intent can be far more powerful if we have chosen it, and certainly if we chose it as a people.

CHAPTER FOURTEEN

Core Essence

The art of staying in your intent supports you in gently moving even deeper into the level of your own core essence. Energetically, the connection between these two is old. If the purpose of your presence on this earth is to live in your truth and it is your intent that supports that happening, connecting with your intent, your Hara, is the first step into the essence of your soul. It is here, in your essence, at this deepest level that you are living purely and in the undefended truth of who you are.

Within this level there is no fear, and, as a result, the willingness to take risks is a natural occurrence. For a soul that has always been, and always will be, what is there to fear? In this depth of your being, there is also an awareness that is physical, energetic, and spiritual, a cellular knowing that whatever you came here to do will be provided for, whatever it is that you will need in order to achieve that goal will be made available.

As an embodied soul, you are an intrinsically pure, holy, and good being, who is a unique reflection of all that is holy. Your true Self is your unique reflection of the Divine. In this aspect of the undefended self, you are all that you will ever need to be. The task is to bring this element of who you are out into the world. Many of those in your life now mirror back to you your fears, your defenses, your lower self, and your wounds. What if those in your life were to mirror back your essence as intrinsically holy and unlimited? Can you imagine what a world you would live in?

I truly believe that we are already everything that we will ever need to be. The great difficulty you may be having is in believing in yourself and trusting that what you know and who you are is real. When you cannot recognize your truth, your own essence, you try to believe your illusions of toughness, of strength, or even an artificial image of being "evolved." You turn to your ego which says "better than" or "holier than" to support a sense of importance in this world. The true self, the true purpose, does not need illusion to recognize its value.

Look at the innocence of children. Their healthy egos allow them to tell you how beautiful they are in a new dress—and they believe it. They will tell you they can throw the ball over the whole house—and they believe it. Their innocence and goodness is real, and it is not measured as against another, only as a reflection of the self. It is a reflection of who they truly are. In some, you see their innocence, in others their goodness and kindness, and in still others their wisdom. These are the qualities of their unique soul, their unique expression of the Divine. As undefended beings, they are able to reflect to the world all that is holy about themselves without discomfort or embarrassment.

As they grow and attempt, with some difficulty, to adapt to this physical world, they appear to develop the need for illusion, the need to prove they deserve to be loved, or to be special. As their fears increase, so does their disconnection from the Self, their embodied soul. Energetically, they are being impacted by those around them, and unfortunately they adapt.

Thankfully, they never lose that innate innocence, that goodness and kindness, or even that wisdom—they may simply lose the pure expression of those qualities. It is their **connection** to that purity that gets lost and yet it can, in time, be rediscovered, if and when they choose to risk letting go of the illusions and the defenses that are blocking it. For some, however, while struggling to learn to live their truth in a world that sees humans as other than holy, they will eventually learn simply to mirror other wounded beings, permanently losing more of their connection to themselves.

Each of you does this to a different degree and in a different way. Learning, as adults, to come home to the essence of the soul that you have always been, learning to listen to that soul as it speaks energetically through your body, is the challenge of personal growth. It requires releasing the pain of your past and letting go of your fears for the future. Eckhart Tolle has said it so clearly—that living in the moment, not the past or the future, is the best approach to living in your truth.

Letting go of illusions, blame, lack, anger, or rage, in regard to the past, and claiming your life in the present, supports you in experiencing what your reality is at this moment—who you are in this moment. Without self-blame or blaming another, just spend a moment, if you can, in a body that has no holding, no pain, and no fear. If you spend time in this place, you may recognize that it is a state of being in which you feel unlimited and unafraid. You feel more you and less encumbered than you feel at any other time. There is a cellular knowing that things are as they were meant to be.

When you drop below all the means by which you have learned not to be at home in your body, you begin to experience the true joy of your soul's qualities. You begin to remember who you are, and have always been. At this point, you can again claim true peace, true joy, and, thankfully, true, unconditional love, all of which, you deserve to experience daily.

Your Soul's Journey

Although there are certainly those who question the existence of a soul, the existence of your core essence apart from your personality, there are also those who are coming to understand its existence in ways they never thought possible. Amazingly, more and more so-called mainstream practitioners are now discussing, if not accepting, the concept of reincarnation. Some older cultures have always accepted this reality; perhaps it is as we age as a culture that we are naturally beginning to accept this on a larger scale, as well.

People such as Brian Weiss, a psychiatrist, who wrote *Many Lives, Many Masters* and *Only Love is Real,* was confronted with the need to address the possibility of past lives because of events taking place in his office with patients who were undergoing hypnosis. After years of exploring the phenomena, he started to write of his and his patients' experiences. Another practitioner, Michael Newton, wrote of stories he collected from his patients undergoing hypnosis as well. In his book, *Journey of Souls: Case Studies of Life Between Lives,* Newton talks about the protocol used in those periods between lives, rather than the multiple-lives themselves. These are all stories relayed to him repeatedly by patients who did not know each other.

For some readers, accepting all of this as unquestionably real may be more than they are able to do at this moment, but the seemingly authentic stories of patients and practitioners may seriously cause them to question what is real. As someone who was raised in a strict Irish Catholic culture, I was certainly never exposed to the concept of past lives. When I first read about the idea as an adult in graduate school, I discounted it as an illusion educated people, and certainly people of faith, did not accept. It made no sense.

During some of my initial training in Energy Medicine, however, I had experiences, or recalls, that I could not explain. In my body, they felt completely real. I did not doubt for a moment the authenticity of my physical experiences, yet intellectually I kept trying to convince myself that they were illusions because I could not fit these experiences into anything I knew as fact. I also did not want to accept them because it would mean changing my whole perspective of life as I knew it and my sense of my soul and the afterlife.

It wasn't until I actually started seeing the past lives of patients that I finally had to accept the possibility of this phenomena being real. Still, I wanted scientific proof, or perhaps validity, so I could consider myself as being intelligent, educated, and grounded. At this point, however, all that we know about this possibility has been acquired through anecdotal research such as the above. I believe we are a long way from having empirical data to prove the existence of past lives and even further from such data that will be readily accepted. As someone who has done extensive research for graduate degrees, including a doctoral dissertation, I am aware that even if we did have the empirical data, as with much of the research that demonstrates evidence of non-traditional findings, any possible empirical data would be held in contempt or ridicule by those who do not want to consider the option regardless of the research results.

However, because of my continued "unusual experiences" for myself, my clients, and my students, I have come to accept that this phenomenon is real and I now work from that perspective. There is great comfort in that realization. We are like infants in our understanding of the world and our place in it. Stretching our view of reality requires a healthy dose of skepticism, but, in addition to an open mind that is willing to acknowledge the possibility of new realities, not instead of. If we don't take the risk, we subject ourselves to a stagnant and righteous existence. I prefer to take a leap of faith.

That being said, in having lived multiple life journeys, the richness and the awareness that is achieved from those experiences exists within your core essence, your soul's essence, as well as within the unconscious aspects of your mind. Your past experiences from those lives as well as the earlier experiences of this journey influence your opinions and your thinking in the current moment. For all that is good, celebrate it. If some results of those experiences are limiting you, you need to look at what the fears are about in your life today, and how you can resolve the issues of both your past and present simultaneously. Your memories, even past life memories, are embedded in your cells and can be remembered and/or resolved. Your journeys, and how you experienced them, are a part of what has made you who you are today on both a personality and soul level. Each journey offers you the opportunity to claim more of who you are, so that you may mirror that back to the world around you, supporting the transformation of the planet.

With each journey, and each moment of this journey, you have additional opportunities to grow, to live fully, passionately, and vibrantly from the purest aspect of who you are. Free will permits you the choice to make that decision or not. Walking the spiritual path, reclaiming your connection to your soul's essence, isn't necessarily easy, yet it is simple—go forward or not, grow or not, simple but not easy. If you choose the first option, the results are a deeper and more powerful understanding and accepting of yourself and of those who have walked the journey with you. You end up with ready access to the "you" that has always existed.

You may leave your core essence at times and go back into fear or illusion; it is a part of the process. Rather than getting lost in the old way of life, however, as with any path you walk frequently, you begin to develop a familiar routine of knowing how to return to your truth more readily and with far less difficulty. You create a path in the sand, and the grass, that leads you home, naturally. You reconnect, then, with the ability to hear your soul's song and to dance to your own rhythm, listening to the words and the melody of your unique musical arrangement. Living every life with joy and celebration is our birth right.

CHAPTER FIFTEEN

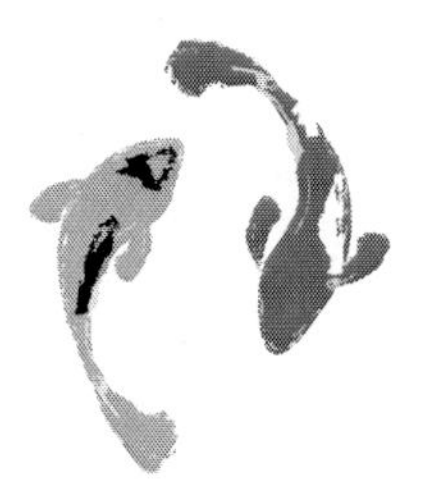

Chakras

In covering for you, to some depth, the various levels of your existence as an embodied soul, I have also shown you the impact of your wounds, resentments, and choices on your ability to remain at the level that is most you, "your best self" as Oprah would say. Understanding the process is a gift, knowing what to do to strengthen or heal it is even better.

Because it is your energy that gets blocked and your health that is later impacted when things are not as you need them to be, understanding the pragmatic, and predictable, energy patterns in your body is important. There is a science to energy flows, and we have a variety of types. The chakras are one group of energy centers that can be easily understand and adjusted if you are willing to support your own health on this level. Accordingly, I would like to offer you some understanding of how they work, what each chakra governs, and the part they have in your healing, thus allowing your soul to sing even more loudly.

Our knowledge of the chakra system is a result of influences from other faiths, other cultures, and other world views. Having the world become a smaller reality than you ever imagined before, readily available international travel has supported you in learning from the richness of other cultures. Your view of your body, your expanded understanding of the multi-dimensional realities of who you are is a gift you have received from those of other cultures. The blending of the best of eastern and western cultures supports you not only in understanding the lives of others, but in understanding yourself and your own body as well.

There has been a great deal written about the chakras by a wide variety of authors coming from various professions and backgrounds. Because each of them sees or senses through their own gifts and their own personalities, to a small degree there are slight differences of opinions as to location or significance of various chakras. At times, this type of "inconsistency" causes some of my students to get lost in confusion when they are looking for the one right answer. For those with more of a Rigid structure, there is a need to know and understand perfectly and seeming contradictions makes them very nervous, if not frustrated and angry.

To make it easy on yourself, if that tendency toward rigidity is your style, it serves you to acknowledge that the slight variations in presentation really do not change the intrinsic quality of what is written. As a practitioner, when you learn to trust what you sense, and trust your ability to know what is needed, the experience of the moment is really what supports the particular healing you are doing.

In graduate school, we read of a leader in psychology who once said something similar to "Learn everything you can learn and then forget everything you know." The meaning is that you should strive to acquire all the knowledge you can, and then, when you are done with an extended period of learning, forget what you know and hold onto the wisdom you have achieved via that amount of knowledge you have embodied.

Understanding the major energy centers in your body can give you a whole new perspective on your health, your body, and your journey. The details can vary, as with everything in life and often-times the different interpretations have limited significance since you fill in your own details as you see and/or experience them. Having a broad understanding supports you in opening your mind and your heart to another perspective and to another level of self-awareness and self-care.

Healthy chakras, which may range normally from 4 to 6 inches in diameter, spin in a clockwise motion acting as funnels for energy coming in and out of the body. Having them uncluttered, as with all the energy flows in your body, supports your health on all levels. As you will see in the explanations below, each chakra has its own qualities.

When you understand how the chakras interact—the psychodynamics between them and the purpose they serve in both maintaining and reclaiming your health—you begin to see them as an invaluable tool for diagnosing and healing. My first-year students learn to read chakras before and after a healing simply so that they can have validation for the changes they have helped support through the healing itself. In their second year, the students are taught how to measure and assess the chakras, as well as to observe the psychodynamic interactions between the various chakras.

A number of books in the New Age sections of the bookstores also discuss the Aura, or auric field. Briefly, the auric field can be seen as a by-product of the chakras. As a result, I will briefly describe the auric field to help you understand how the chakras support it. As you will see below, each chakra has a different color that resonates with its vibration. In addition, each of the chakras radiates energy out of the body, thereby creating an energy field which surrounds the body similar to a cocoon with each layer of the field immediately over the other, creating a seven layer reality, the auric field, with each layer being a different color.

The first chakra creates the first level of the auric field, wrapping around your entire body; this is the layer closest to your physical body. The second chakra creates the second level of your field and it is just after the first, the 2nd layer away from your physical body. The third chakra creates the third level of the field and so forth. To understand how this energy field looks, if you cannot see it and do not have Kirlian photography available, here is a brief explanation.

If you tend to be very fragile and prone to getting lost in books rather than physical activity, you may have very little energy in your first chakra since your energy is located more in the cerebral 6th and 7th chakras. As a result, the first layer of your energy field will be very thin, perhaps ½"thick. If instead, you are very athletic and involved in extensive sports activities, you may have a disproportionate amount of energy in your first chakra (very physical) and, as a result, the first level of your auric field may be significantly larger, perhaps 6 or more inches thick, creating a thick red glow seen in special photography called Kirlian photography. If you are healthy, the color glows; if you're unhealthy, it may be more dull or heavy in texture. Where and how you hold your energy defines not only how your chakras function, but the density and make-up of your auric field as well.

This isn't good or bad, it just is. In addition, because there are seven **major** chakras (you also have many smaller chakras throughout your body), there are seven levels to your auric field, each one just past the other, similar to the layers of an onion. Since the odd numbered layers, 1, 3, 5, and 7 are structured, they feel very different from 2, 4, and 6, which are progressively more diffused.

Let me describe some of the color sequencing of the chakra system and the auric field:

- The color of the first level of your field, regardless of thickness, is red as is the color of the first chakra
- The second level of the field is orange as is the color of the energy in your second chakra. If you tend to be highly emotional, this layer of your field will be very thick. If you do not have a lot of emotional energy and tend to be more pragmatic and responsive rather than reactive, this layer may be very thin
- The third level of the field is yellow. If you tend to be more intellectual, a "thinker," this level of the field will be thick since you hold so much energy in that area. If you speak before you think and react from emotion rather than respond from logic, this layer may be very thin
- This process continues up through the seven levels of the field
- A necessary point to remember, however, is that because the even numbered levels of the field are progressively more diffused, progressively thinner in substance, they can look like clouds of various colors, or even, for the 6th level, a mist of various colors.

How a practitioner sees them depends on many factors. Sometimes they can appear all white or grey. The colors can be vibrant, pastel, or very dull. So much depends upon you, your physical health, your vibrancy, depression, and so many other influences. Blocks in the field can appear to be thickened or dense areas; they blend in yet they don't. Dramatically different in appearance, your soul's essence radiates with brilliant colors that just expand all around you in a powerful, awe-inspiring, and compelling way.

In regard to the chakras themselves, generally speaking, there are elements that relate to all the chakras, even though each is unique.

- Each chakra corresponds to specific body parts and functions, and is both impacted by and impacts specific psycho/spiritual beliefs related to its area
- Each, when healthy, flows clockwise and can average about 6" in diameter
- When there are thoughts, fears, traumas, or emotions held inside a chakra, these will impact the flow of the energy going in or out, and, if the holding is sustained or increased, physical disease or disorders can result
- A simple exercise of spinning the chakras yourself each morning or evening can help support your energetic and, ultimately, your physical, emotional, and spiritual health.

Plate 1: Picture showing The Chakras (with Related Sanskrit Symbols)**, the Aura, the radiance of the Core Essence, and rainbow-colored Layers of the Field**

Chakra Qualities

First Chakra: This is red and is located at the very bottom of the torso. This reflects:

- Your right to exist on the physical plane—to survive
- Your right to security and safety
- Your need to possess/own
- Your need to belong to a group or family
- If balanced, it supports prosperity, health, and belonging to a group or place—claiming your right to a strong and solid presence here on earth
- Problems that may occur when the first chakra is unbalanced are skin, muscle, bone, joint, and ligament diseases or disorders, as well as hysteria and/or anxiety, and hoarding.

Second Chakra: This is orange and is located in the abdomen below the navel. It reflects:

- Your sexuality and passion
- Your emotions
- Your creativity
- Your physical and emotional pleasure
- If balanced, it supports emotional stability, healthy creative flow in all areas, pregnancy, and sexual satisfaction
- If imbalanced, problems that may occur are in the reproductive organs, the immune system, and being overly emotional or emotionally disconnected, as well as addictions, and sexual disorders.

Third Chakra: This is yellow and is located in the solar plexus (base of the rib cage). It reflects:

- Your need for – and belief in – your autonomy
- Your personal power and self-definition—your power/will balance
- Your self-respect and self-confidence
- Your intuition

- If balanced, there is playfulness, spontaneity, self-care, self-discipline, and a comfort with yourself and your personal power
- If unbalanced, potential problems may occur in the liver, gallbladder, pancreas, spleen, or stomach or in disorders such as fibromyalgia and chronic fatigue. Emotionally, when unbalanced there is a tendency toward rage and aggression or the illusion of powerlessness and blaming.

Fourth Chakra: This is green and is located near the heart. It reflects:

- Your ability to love and to accept love from others
- Your compassion and caring for one other or a group
- Your ability to love unconditionally
- Your being open and accepting
- If balanced, this chakra supports your ability to be in relationship with yourself and others. There is also room for grief, forgiveness, and understanding
- If unbalanced, there is difficulty in giving and/or receiving love. There may be issues with co-dependency in relationships or in letting go and moving on when needed. On the physical level, there may be heart disease, heart attack, lung disorders, breast problems, and upper back difficulties.

Fifth Chakra: This is blue and is located in the throat. It reflects:

- Your ability to speak your truth powerfully, as well as to hear the truth when spoken by others
- Your communication skills
- Your willingness to identify your needs and to speak them so they are heard
- Your creativity in expressing who you are
- If balanced, it supports your ability to be fully seen and heard in your life, as well as your ability to hear others in their own self-expression
- If unbalanced, you may fear speaking your truth, or, conversely, force your opinion on others. Physically there is a tendency to sore throats, laryngitis, TMJ, swollen glands, gum or teeth disorders, and thyroid problems.

Sixth Chakra: This is indigo and is located in the center of the forehead. It reflects:

- Your ability to visualize your dreams
- Your psychic vision
- Your ability to see the big picture, the spiritual significance
- Your intellectual capabilities
- Your willingness to see other perspectives
- Your ability for creative imagination
- If balanced, there is the ability for emotional and intellectual intelligence and an openness to what cannot be seen or planned. You can see and accept the interchange between the spiritual and physical realms in day-to-day life
- If unbalanced, there is a tendency for headaches of all types, nightmares, hallucinations, brain disorders, sight difficulties, and learning disabilities.

Seventh Chakra: This is violet or white and is located at the crown of the head. It reflects:

- Your ability to identify and hold onto your universal wisdom
- Your expanded consciousness
- Your ability to trust life, knowing you are guided
- Your ethics and integrity
- Your faith and spirituality
- Your capacity to see and know that you are a part of a greater reality than your own
- Your sense of being a global citizen
- If balanced, you live in a knowing that is both physical and spiritual. You have the Self and the Other in your consciousness
- If unbalanced, you can get caught in spiritual desolation, and/or feeling disconnected or forgotten. You can become either overly intellectual or lost in confusion and misunderstanding.

As you can see, they are in the order of the colors of the rainbow due to vibrational levels, starting with the heaviest and moving through to the lightest flow, red, orange, yellow, green, blue, indigo, and violet.

Let me explain how the symbolism of each chakra works in unison with the others, so that you can see that, once you choose to be fully embodied and claim your place on this planet, you will be able to take care of your health and your physical body and become an active part of your community (1st).

With that commitment in place, you are then ready to own all of your emotions, your sexuality, and your creativity. You are physically here, so now you are claiming your emotional health, as well. When you are doing so, your creativity leaves you open for the creation of another life, as well as for creating the journey you chose to undertake. Unfortunately for many, some choose to begin relationships from this level, before they are aware of who they truly are. What they bring to the relationship and what they expect is limited to what they are aware of at this point in their existence; as a result, the relationships originating from this chakra are based primarily on lust or emotional neediness. Consequently, love is confused with emotional attachment, and respect is confused with neediness, enmeshment, and co-dependency. Some can develop along with their partner after this premature decision, but many cannot. When this chakra is functioning well, your immune system is strengthened because all of who you are is coming into its own and you are at peace with your life as you created it (2nd).

Now that you have committed to being here, and you are claiming the emotional and creative elements of who you are, you begin to have a sense of your own personal power, and are claiming your intuitive knowing, so that your self-confidence is in place as you claim your own autonomy, taking responsibility for the decisions you make in your life and in your unfolding (3rd).

Once you have achieved that level of autonomy and you are established in your life and your self-care, you are now ready to enter a healthy relationship with another. Because of your confidence and your sense of self, there is the ability to be independent while intimately opening your heart to another and to the world around you with compassion and caring, allowing your heart energy to flow freely and joining with others in a shared vision (4th).

Being comfortable in your skin, emotionally, and sexually at home with who you are, ready to take responsibility and ownership for your decisions, open and ready for a relationship, and to be a compassionate member of your community, you feel comfortable acknowledging what you need to go forward and speaking about it with those whom you love and who are in relationship with. Claiming your voice, and hearing what others have to say as well, supports you in being an active and intimate part of the whole, with a voice in how that looks (5th).

Having reached this level of belonging, being in both intimate and communal relationships where you are all able to speak your truth and be heard, you are able to plan for the future, visualizing a dream for your life, for who you are becoming—and for making it happen (6th).

Once that level of physical involvement in the journey occurs, and you have been balanced in the process, you will have acquired sufficient wisdom and the intellectual development necessary for your journey at any given moment. Because of experience gained, you can see the patterns in your life and learn from them, knowing this is most definitely a spiritual journey you are walking (7th).

Because we are human, none of us who are still walking this journey are able to stay balanced at all times. As a practitioner, with clients I may see on a regular basis, I notice the few chakras that are generally balanced and flowing freely as that person's standard. I can also see those chakras that are usually the first to go out of balance when that particular client gets stressed. It is their pattern; it is their way of dealing or not dealing with stressors. That is their human experience. It can be worked with and supported.

Your coming to understand how you respond or react to stress will support you in being able to know what you need for self-care at those times. We all have stress. We all have conflict and disappointments that come into our lives. How you deal with each of these defines the patterns of energy flow you develop. Knowing, now, that you have the ability to control the flow makes it a possible and necessary aspect of self-care. You need to be willing to make that commitment.

Notice that with all of these chakras, there is the ability to be fed multi-dimensionally, as well as the ability to be impacted negatively and multi-dimensionally. Each chakra works independently, yet also as a part of the whole. As an example, because the earth energy comes up through the first chakra, if that is closed or at 1" in diameter, there may be minimal flow throughout the entire system. As a practitioner, I have seen that when you are able to open the first chakra, there can be an amazing sensation. It is as if you have opened a faucet, and immediately the energy is pouring in under your hands. It is a wonderful sensation.

For clients who are attuned to their bodies, and can experience their own energy flows, it can be a time of great joy and feeling alive; for a practitioner, as the energy goes through your client's body, you are able to better experience or see the areas that are blocked, or lethargic, or holding themselves still, as well as those areas where the energy is flowing freely. It tells you a great deal about where to work in supporting your client in coming into balance.

Theoretically, you can work up the body, from the feet to the crown, opening up each chakra as you go, yet this is where the art of this science comes into play. It is an art that is more easily developed when you have had sufficient training because of the knowledge and wisdom you have acquired through both lectures and supervised practice. This added benefit of extensive training is that the client is supported by someone who truly understands all that is taking place. For the practitioner, the real joy of this work is experienced as you become energetically intimate with each client, understanding how their energy body works, perhaps even better than they understand that. You receive the gift of being able to teach them and show them what they may have missed in their belief and in the modern life style of struggle and rush.

In following through with the case example from above, once that first chakra opens, it is not uncommon to need to do special exercises or to have a healer assist in opening the second chakra, if it has been held closed for a long period of time partially due to a lack of energy flow. Once that is completed and the client is coming into an acceptance of their emotions and their passion, for life as well as sexually, they may start to feel alive again and be thrilled at the experience. They also may become frightened and close both their 1st and 2nd chakras down immediately, since having both open may be too overwhelming and admitting more life force than they are comfortable with.

This dynamic requires the skill of being extra sensitive to what is happening within the client. I have literally had clients *say* to me, "I don't care if you need to break a bone to get this block removed, please help me, I want to move on." What I *hear* is, "My will centers, my ego, and my frustration want growth now; please force my psyche, my body, and my mind to go along." Ethically, unless this client, in a fully embodied way, is ready for the change, I am abusing them by forcing them to go where they are not ready to go. Once they are fully ready, they will open and stay open—with the smallest amount of focused and grounded energy available—without a battle of the wills.

Unconditional love, an ability to share some of the insights the practitioner has received, and a little more time may allow the client to be fully ready to move on and to be finished with whatever was holding him or her back. My statistics and/or my ego as a practitioner should never have more importance than the client's natural timeline.

Another experience I have observed more than once is that when a client opens their second chakra fully, they will then, unconsciously, close the fourth chakra in reaction to that opening. To observe that dynamic tells the healer that there may be a fear or vulnerability in this particular client in regard to having both 2 and 4 open at the same time. Perhaps they can be sexually open with someone, but to open up their heart fully at the same time makes them too vulnerable to having their heart broken. To be that open or invested may lead them to fear that they will be controlled or abused by another. Watching the dynamics tells us a lot, but we always need to go back to the client to get the specific details, since each individual is different and has his or her own unique experiences and fears, as well as his or her own reaction to them.

Along those same lines, I have noticed that when someone finally gets to open his or her third chakra and claim their personal power after a great deal of effort and personal growth, s/he may then close the fifth chakra, sometimes firmly, and sometimes just for a few moments until we work with providing unconditional love and acceptance for this newly empowered soul who is leaving its wounds behind. By working on the fifth chakra, with the intent of supporting the person in the ability to speak from this new-found power and to honor it without fear of offending another, s/he is able to start feeling at home in the body. It may take some time and practice, but keeping both open can best support that person's stepping up to the plate for self and others.

To support greater balance in your life and in your actions, focusing specifically on a day-to-day basis on the interplay between the second chakra emotions, the fourth chakra and your heart, and the sixth chakra with your brain, allows you to keep your emotions flowing, your heart open, and your brain present providing balance in all your interactions. Excessive energy in any of these can cause you to become more emotional than you intended, have your heart respond without insight and cause you to commit more than you logically can, or have your brain coldly analyze a situation without the balance of a loving heart.

You may or may not have noticed it, but, as I said earlier, truth is truth and we can approach it and speak of it in any number of ways. If you remember what you read about the character structures being multi-dimensional and dealing with the many aspects of who you are, you will find that the traits that we discussed in the structures, such as the Creative/Schizoid having great difficulty being embodied and feeling safe, reflects very much on the same issues of the first chakra with the same propensity for disorders. Working from this understanding of the chakra interrelationships is simply another way of approaching the same issues in the same person, multi-dimensionally.

The second chakra issues of needing to deal with one's needs, emotions, and possible addictions relate in many ways to the Empathic/Oral structure. I could go on, but I believe you can see the point.

The more approaches you can take to understanding what is happening with you—or with your clients, if you are a practitioner—the better chance you have of fully resolving what issues may exist and/or supporting what strengths you or your clients possess for personal health and for the journey. As a therapist, if my client does not hear what I am saying one way, I will simply rephrase it, or give that client an example from my life, since it can be so much easier to see things in another, at times. Again, if after three attempts they do not see it, I back away and let the client get it in his or her own time. Otherwise, it can become a battle of the wills, and many have that everywhere they go. It ends up with no winners, and a need to prevail for its own sake is unhealthy in any case.

There are times in working with the chakras of clients that I have found things neither of us ever would have expected. It is at these moments when I remind myself that the leaps of faith I have taken need to be repeated often. If I stay in integrity, and stay grounded and present in the moment, I have come to trust that whatever happens, I will be fine, and this is just another chance to step out of the box and move forward along my path. Also, I believe that when an agreement to grow is heard by Spirit, the opportunities for growth keep coming.

If things were always safe and non-challenging, they wouldn't necessarily be growth producing. The more often you consent to grow and become who you are meant to be, the more experiences will come into your life calling you to respond in ways you never knew were possible. You discover a confidence, a sense of self you had only hoped for, and an increasing willingness to really live this life since merely surviving it would feel like a long, protracted death. It's a great thing we acquire confidence with age as well, since over time many of us have walked, whether by choice or happenstance, the road less traveled by those we have known.

Chakra Difficulties

I had one woman come into my office due to abdominal pain that just wouldn't go away regardless of the medications she took or diet she followed. When I asked what had been happening in her life she told me that she had made a commitment to herself to never enter into a sexual relationship again in her life. As far as she was concerned, her second chakra was dead. She told me that she had been in many relationships and usually became sexually active almost immediately within those. A few months into these relationships, she usually found out that she didn't like the person of the moment at all and had no idea why she ever started dating him in the first place. To her way of thinking, she had finally found the perfect solution—not dating. What I suggested was that perhaps she could date people for a few months **before** becoming sexually active, and then, when she did involve herself sexually she would know who she was going to be with.

That idea made no sense to her, so she asked instead for energy work to help solve the physical problem. Rarely do one-dimensional healings occur on demand, but I was willing to see where this would take us. Amazingly, as I got to the second chakra, I felt called to go deeper into this work than usual. I stabilized myself and allowed my energy to follow where it was being led. Energetically, I put my hands inside the second chakra, between the pubic bone and the navel, and instinctively cupped my hands to remove something that I sensed was there and needed to come out. As I put my hands in, I felt something very soft and warm. As I pulled them out, I saw that there was an opossum hiding in her second chakra. It was rolled up in a ball shape, and yet the belly, which was resting on my hands, was very soft and warm. It was like holding an infant. My heart was touched by the sweetness of this creature. As with anything energetic that is removed from the body, I held it up to be taken to the spiritual realm. As I watched it moving away, I was struck by the vision of this creature changing shape into that of a man and returning home to the spiritual realm.

In choosing to play dead, she had called energy similar to her own into that area of her body within which she was playing dead. This man had been one who played dead in his life. Not all souls cross over at the time of death, for a number of reasons. In situations where they are later ready to go home to the world of spirit, they will piggyback on someone who has similar energy or is dealing with a similar situation to theirs. This was one of those situations. However, because she was aware of this work and aware of her own body, my client was open to whatever it took to begin her healing. After this spiritual extraction, she changed her mind about dating and sexuality, and was willing to try my suggestion when she was ready to date again. The cost of playing dead was too high and out of her truth.

Another client of mine presented with knee problems that were lifelong, although, in her thirties, her knees were becoming more painful and less flexible than she wanted to accept. Because the problems were lifelong, I was aware that there was a possibility that there were some past life issues present. As I began working with her left knee, I became aware that we would definitely be doing past life work. I first worked with the problems of this lifetime, such as falls she had taken, landing on her knees. When the healing in both knees felt complete for this period, I was led to another time, where I saw her in the woods and observed that she had fallen off her horse. She was wearing the clothes appropriate for that period. After she fell, her horse bucked and one hoof landed on her knee.

This was the knee that in this lifetime was the weaker of the two. I again dealt with both knees, but was required to spend considerably more time on the crushed knee, while energetically reconstructing the joint as best I could, calling in all the help I could receive. When I had done as much as I could, I waited to see if we were now finished with this healing. I was then led to one last lifetime of hers to work on this issue. My first sensation was the smell of cobblestone and horses. After that, I heard noises that sounded as if there were many people present in this place. Finally, I saw that we were in a town square and my client was lying on the ground.

It appeared that she had been crucified, but that thick stakes had been pounded through her knees and hands into the ground—an alternative to nailing her to an upright cross. Wood had been scarce. She had died there. When I removed the stakes from her knees, I saw that one of her knees had become badly infected and turned gangrenous before she had died. Again, the more damaged, gangrenous knee was the one that manifested as her weaker knee in this lifetime. After we had completed that work as best I could with reconstruction and healing, we were finished with our work for the day. She reported a month after that healing that her knees were doing remarkably well, and she had had no further pain or discomfort. When a practitioner begins a healing, he or she has only a general idea as to where it will lead, and, even at that, it is imperative to be aware that it may go in a completely different direction.

Because our body knows what it needs far more than does our conscious mind, it is far better that the body leads. I have found, consistently, that it allows a client to find a connection to his or her soul—the essence that s/he had been missing. You are led where you need to go, and your soul inevitably takes you by way of the path that best teaches you what it is that you came on this journey to learn. As an integral aspect of health care, that path supports a true healing every time, even if no cure takes place. Sometimes disease is the route back to spirit, and the dying process can be a gift of closure and completion. If so, we simply help the process be as peaceful and fruitful as possible.

Watching death take place, when a patient has allowed you to support him or her on that journey, can be an extremely mystical experience. A number of my students have done their medical internships in hospice settings and have had their lives and their healerships transformed by the experience. Not only do you get to experience others coming to greet the passing soul, you can begin to see, sense, or feel his or her chakras almost evaporating as s/he leaves the first one, then the second, and so forth. Because the first chakra is about our embodiment, when it is time for the embodied soul to leave, that is the first chakra to close and then disappear from sight. The soul can be seen leaving, usually from the upper chakras, the throat area, or the crown. The chakras, our energetic centers for this physical form, are no longer needed, and, therefore, as the soul leaves, they disintegrate.

When infants enter this world, their chakras are not balanced due to the need to become acclimated to this physical journey. Their first chakras may be ¼" while the 7th may be 12"– 15" because they are still very much a part of the spiritual world. It is only once they begin to recognize their physical movements, the ability to touch or to bring someone's attention to him or herself that they actually begin to acknowledge the reality of their physical existence and their role in it. Accordingly, at about that time the 1st chakra starts to expand and the 7th begins to decrease, since more of the energy is now being called into the lower areas of the body to support their physical embodiment and survival.

The opposite occurs at death when there is no longer a need for the physical, or lower, chakras. For many who are preparing for death, the 6th and 7th chakras open far more than they had been throughout life and, as a result, the ability to see those on the other side who are familiar is a common occurrence. For many, fortunately, this makes the passing less frightening and even comforting.

CHAPTER SIXTEEN

Cellular Memory

Finally, in doing all you can in bringing your energetic body, your emotions, your spirituality, and your thoughts into alignment, there is the reality of your cellular memory, a memory that encompasses all of these elements listed above and so much more. Your cells hold your past and present; even when your body seems to be forgetting how to function, your cells remember.

Researchers in dance therapy have shown that seniors who are wheelchair-bound, unable to walk on their own, upon hearing music from the '40s, can get up on the dance floor and dance through an entire song while later, when the music stops, need to be helped back to their chairs. Their cells remembered the emotion, the steps, and the experience, and helped them do the "impossible." These are areas of research that I find intriguing and very exciting. Our bodies are such wondrous creations.

In reviewing articles on cellular memory listed in Google Scholar, 602,000 articles were listed - 602,000, can you imagine? Clearly, the concept, although perhaps new to some, has been a topic of significant research. Rather than reviewing and translating the research here, I simply want to share my excitement and the extent to which the field has been explored. In *The Heart's Code* Pearsall writes:

> An irrational world brings us only misery, but a millennium in which the gifted brain is moderated and instructed by a gentle heart could bring us a shared paradise on earth. If we are willing to try to combine the best the brain has created, and will create, with the wisdom of the heart's code that may be our soul calling

> out the cellular memories that give meaning to these creations, we can become much smarter than we have ever been. We can have two major intelligences and learn to adore the rational skepticism of science and still look for the energy of the soul conveyed by the heart. (p.17)

If ever there was an arena where the combined strengths of your heart and your brain could come into play, this is that arena. Every experience of your journey is locked in every cell of your being. Every interpretation, as well as the resultant pain or joys of those interpretations of your experiences, are locked in every cell of your body. In reviewing what has been written in this book thus far, the three levels of your existence, including your masks, your defenses, your wounds, your lower self, your core wound, and your soul's essence, are all locked in each and every cell of who you are. What an awareness that is!

Doesn't that explain the phantom pain of the amputee? Why and how does the arm or leg feel pain when it doesn't even exist? What of the terror still in someone who has escaped a horrific experience and who is now in a safe and caring environment? If you have ever been with someone in terrible emotional pain as they rock themselves, whether to escape or to assimilate what has just happened, you can see the experience as it exists throughout their entire system. It is not just his or her heart that hurts. It does not just confuse their brain. Their entire body, every cell, is in shock, denial, and grief.

It is a complete body experience that requires healing of the entire body. It has impacted every aspect of who he or she is. If you are a practitioner, bringing both your heart and your brain to that healing is the gift you have to offer. Combining what you know from whatever training you may have had with what you can feel in your heart allows your heart, your soul, and your brain to be a part of the unconditional support and caring you can provide as one human being, one embodied soul, to another.

This level of healing is instinctual. Everything in you, if you are undefended and have an open heart, calls you to be there for another in such a condition whether you are a practitioner or not. Is it because it causes you to remember your own painful moments and the needs you had at that time? Is it because of a universal knowing, a universal memory, an archetypal memory, an empathic moment when the illusion of "other" is removed and the recognition that we are all one comes alive? In that undefended state, regardless of the cause, every cell in your body wants to be there to support another. That is the loving expression of one embodied soul, one open, loving heart, walking this journey with another.

The above is only one way in which you can be there for another. Your sharing of the journey can now also happen in ways that fifty years ago would have seemed impossible except for those with wonderfully, far-thinking, creative, and heart-infused minds. The miracle of transplant surgery is still in its infancy and yet we have learned amazing things about both the scientific and heart-based components of this process. Scientifically, surgeons are perfecting their abilities in the transplanting of increasingly more organs; in addition, the numbers and types of organs that can be transplanted continue to increase. Who knows what the future holds as medicine continues to expand the capabilities of those who practice it?

It is both the manual, pragmatic application of medicine that is continuing to grow as well as the need for a deeper and more invested heart-based approach to this work. The field of medicine is growing into realms that require additional skills. The emphasis on the art and science of medicine needs to become more balanced. Both have always been needed and both have always been brought there by those who innately bring each to the table as well as by those who, with experience, have come to see the many levels of skill required in spite of their learning. The work nonetheless now requires discovering more and more about the intangible qualities of concepts such as energy, cellular memory, and the soul.

A courageous woman named Claire Sylvia wrote her book *A Change of Heart: A Memoir* perhaps to inspire others in need of transplant surgery as well as to encourage those who may be willing to donate their organs. Her story of receiving the hearts and lungs of a teenager killed in a motorcycle accident brings the awareness of cellular memory to a new and very personal level. Having a deadly disease and needing a transplant, she had no idea what her life would be like after the procedure. As the first heart/lung recipient in New England, she also had no past histories to lean on for support.

What she discovered made the physical implications of her recovery the least complicated aspect of her climb back into health, although certainly none of the process could be considered easy. In the days and months that followed, Claire came to realize that she received so much more from her donor than just his physical organs. She also received his tastes, his sensations, and his memories. Having been very much a woman of the good life, she had enjoyed the best accommodations when traveling and the best quality food. After her surgery, she craved Chicken McNuggets™ and had a desire to back-pack throughout Europe. Her friends felt this was a result of the trauma of her near death and the surgery. She knew better.

After a great deal of research, she discovered that the organs she had received came from a young man saving to go back-packing through Europe with his friends. He had been killed in a motorcycle accident on the way home from work with his favorite food, Chicken McNuggets™, in his leather jacket. In addition to realizing that these new tastes and these new sensations were those of her donor, she realized as well that some of the memories she was having were his also.

As one woman who recognized that we are here to serve as well as to be served, Claire brought this information to Bernie Siegel, M.D., who created and still maintains Exceptional Cancer Patient Support Groups. She wanted to begin support groups for transplant recipients to support them in dealing with the implications of what their surgery meant. How would others deal with the realization that the cellular memory, and perhaps an aspect of another's soul, would now co-exist within their body?

How would they deal with knowing that their world, their life experiences, were about to change? She had discovered as a recipient that cellular memory lives long past the death of the physical form. Would the recipients' biases, their judgments, and their spiritual beliefs cause a rejection of the organ because of who it came from? Matching blood type and physical compatibility was a necessity but what of all the other implications as well? Further research on findings such as hers is a necessity if we are to increase the ratio of cases without complications in acceptance vs. rejection.

In another example of cellular memory living past the death of the donor, Pearsall writes of an 8 year old girl who received the heart of a 10 year old girl who had been murdered. The recipient had dreams at night about the man who had killed her donor. When the attending physician and the girl's mother contacted police, they were able to find and arrest the murderer based on the facts provided by the little girl concerning the time, place, and weapon, including the murdered little girl's words to this man.

There are many more stories and very much more to learn. Skeptics can work to dispute the interpretation but, with enough anecdotal information, eventually we will need to accept that perhaps what we need is a new paradigm for research rather than a dismissal of information that is open to inquiry. As one who has been involved in Energy Medicine research both as an administrator and as a primary investigator, I am aware that the concepts of controls and placebos need to be reconsidered. For some, research is now moving into the realm of the non-physical and the non-chemical, and thus past guidelines for physical data collection and placebo comparisons may no longer be adequate or appropriate for the applicable research protocol needed.

Other examples of what may or may not be cellular memory include situations similar to one I had many years ago. I do not know of any scientific explanation although there may be several suppositions. I was sitting in a restaurant which had a small dance floor with a girlfriend on a quiet Friday evening. There was a couple in their mid-thirties on the dance floor dancing to music from a radio. Their style was smooth and flawless and so I watched in admiration. As I watched them leave the dance floor, I was quite impressed with their abilities. However, once they reached the table where they were sitting, something happened.

Without intent, and before I had experience in recognizing the need for self-protection and self-care, I had an experience where I was transferred back, whether through the energy field or perhaps her cellular memory, to when this woman was 3 years of age and was being raped by her father. I could hear her screams as well as feel her trauma, shock, and pain. Before this would end, I quickly went through different intervals when she was older in which this happened repeatedly, until I was finally in the recent past and saw or sensed that she was an alcoholic and that this relationship she was in was very abusive.

I have now learned very well how to protect myself, how to set boundaries, and yet still, I am curious, as to what happened. Did I tap into her cellular memory? Did I tap into what is regarded as the Akashic Records, the records of all souls' experiences? There are so many possible intelligent guesses but at this point in time there is no one answer that can be proven. If we can open our minds to the scientific research of realties that are beyond the scope of a mechanical approach to science inquiry, we may find answers not yet known to questions that will arise far more frequently by many more practitioners as Energy Medicine is taught and practiced on a larger scale.

Certainly we need to keep guidelines, we need to keep a healthy level of skepticism to help provide an objective assessment, but we also need to have a balance. The goal needs to be to collect findings that can support or dispute a supposition, not to find ways to negate what we do not understand or do not want to accept. Bringing the heart, soul, and brain together may support a more heart and soul-based science with the strengths and insights that each dimension can bring to the table.

Clearly, supporting an ever-changing landscape may require an approach that is as non-linear as the work being done. The *Oxford Dictionary* defines science as:

- A branch of knowledge involving systematized observation and experimentation
- A systematic and formulated knowledge esp. on a specific subject
- A skillful technique.

Each of these descriptions needs to be maintained; interpreting how that happens seems to be the dilemma. What an exciting time to be involved in this work as we progress and move both science and medicine further while adapting to a reality that is not solely mechanically or chemically based and that has room for what some may see as the unseen and the non-obvious.

CHAPTER SEVENTEEN

Quantitative Research in Energy Medicine and Energy Psychology

After the wide variety of experiences I had in this field of spiritually-based wholistic health, my interest in understanding it further, and giving it credibility, came to a head when one of my students asked if I would Co-Chair the Advisory Board of a multi-million dollar Frontier Medicine Grant given by the National Institutes of Health (NIH) to the University of Connecticut. In addition, I was asked to submit a proposal for grant funding to research my work. This work was going to combine the best of Energy Medicine with the new field of energy psychology.

In needing to pick one aspect of my work, one disorder, I chose to do my research with patients who had Fibromyalgia. The reason I chose this disorder was because I saw so many for whom the psychological and spiritual correlates were so obvious and so consistent. This was going to be a concrete study on my beliefs that when we lose touch with our own essence, with who we are meant to be, because of living in reaction to wounds, etc, or in order to be who we "should" be, we not only lose touch with ourselves spiritually, but we also pay a great price emotionally and physically.

My first experience with this disorder was with a psychologist when her disorder, which was not common in the early days, was misdiagnosed as rheumatoid arthritis. She had been placed on anti-inflammatory medication. When she was told this would be for the rest of her life, she became depressed and was placed on anti-depressants. Being one who lived her life in the guidelines of wholistic health, she became very nervous about what all these medications were doing to her body, so they put her on anti-anxiety medication so she could sleep and function. Unfortunately, with all these medications in her body she could sleep but not function.

After working with her for a period of time, I came to see that many of her symptoms were along the bladder meridian (an energetic line running primarily along the spine and down the center/back of your legs) or were referred pain from that area. Combining one half-hour of psychotherapy with one-half hour of table work began to work wonders for her. She was able to begin removing herself, with her doctor's supervision, from the medications until she was only on pain medication as needed.

At that point, I asked her when all this pain had begun. She had never thought about it but told me that it was when her daughter had started talking about doing her junior year of college overseas and was exploring her options. That response began, for me, another area of anecdotal research to follow-up with since I consider point of onset significant in understanding the psycho/spiritual reason for a disorder. As time went on, I continued to get additional training in Energy Medicine while expanding my practice, which had started having increasing numbers of new referrals with physical diseases and disorders.

Because it is not uncommon for parents to fill their own needs in their children, as if the needs of their child were the same as theirs had been, I later asked her how she mothered her daughters. She was quite clear that she protects them "as I should." Protecting them was extremely important to her.

The mother's fears that her daughter would become sad or lonely or wouldn't like the food, the people, or the classes, were based on her fears that the people her daughter would stay with wouldn't like her, comfort her, or accept her. She was really very overly concerned for her daughter. In her daughter's naiveté, as her mother reported it, her daughter couldn't wait to leave. It would be an adventure regardless of what it entailed and it was time-limited.

As I began to ask questions concerning point of onset, I also began to take note of the various personality styles that came into my office and came to recognize patterns of personality and disorder propensity. I have included those previously in the chapters on the character structures. In hearing of Barbara Brennan's book *Hands of Light,* I bought the book and felt even more at home than I had with Jin Shin Do. Here was someone else who had visions and who was in the field of Energy Medicine. After four years of training with Barbara, a NASA scientist and energy medicine practitioner, including a few additional modalities I studied along the way, my understanding of this work and of the emotional and spiritual implications in physiological disease was becoming progressively more solid and being increasingly more validated by the clients.

Louise Hay had released her first version of *You Can Heal Your Life*, showing the psycho/spiritual correlates she perceived to exist in physical disorder and I began to wonder about the hundredth monkey syndrome. Were there really others out there who were also recognizing what I was seeing? The affirmation of what I saw was wonderful, and yet I could not find anything in the scientific papers that addressed these issues so clearly.

However, the field of psychoneuroimmunology generated a movement back to the more traditional understanding of a wholistic perspective in health care while also encouraging the development of extensive research providing clear evidence that our emotions impact our immune and adrenal systems, for both good and bad (Friedman, 1996; Kiecolt-Glaser, Kennedy, Malkoff, Fisher, Speicher, & Glaser, 1988; Pignatelli, Magalhaes, & Magalhaes, 1998; Spiegel, 1997.)

In expanding this work, my objective in doing this research was to assess the emotional and spiritual beliefs of those with Fibromyalgia in regard to how they lived their lives, including their relationships, as well as to understand their approach to dealing with this disorder. I wanted to expand specifically upon the work of others such as Gordon, Merenstein, D'Amico, & Hudgens (1998) in exploring the possibility of energy healing as a multi-dimensional means of healing Fibromyalgia.

There were two primary questions guiding this research: Do specific psycho/spiritual beliefs or pseudo-myths support the development of specific disorders and, if so, can these beliefs be released or changed through Energy Medicine treatment, while also supporting the healing of the physical symptoms?

To participate in this research the individuals needed to be 18 years of age, on pain medications as needed rather than on a standard dosage - if they are drugged not to feel how would they know if they were in pain or not? - and not be on pain medication for any other physical disorder.

We excluded those who had pending litigation for disability related to Fibromyalgia since they would be invested in maintaining their pain and any limitations in order to receive their compensation, as well as excluding those with other medical diagnoses that are known to result in chronic pain. We also excluded those who relied upon the disorder to belong to the only social support groups they had. The intent was to eliminate any biases in honest reporting, thus increasing the validity of the responses.

Past studies in the areas of neuroscience, microbiology, medicine, and psychology have clearly demonstrated a generalized impact of the mind on the nervous, endocrine, and immune systems (Butler, Koopman, Classen, & Spiegel, 1999; DeKeyser, 2003; Dyer, 2002; Gruber, et al., 1993; Pert, 1999). Other studies have shown connections between specific emotional and physiological disorders, such as some recent research that suggests that depression contributes to disease by way of increasing immune dysfunction.

Their research and the writings of Louise Hay, Deborah Shapiro, and others demonstrate how important it is to understand that your personality style, your emotions, your beliefs, and how you hold your energy, impact your physical health. As an example, frequent or sustained anger has been explored, including the body's reaction to anger, such as turbulent blood flow, fat being released into the bloodstream for energy during an angry episode, along with the resultant development of atherosclerotic plaque formation. Each of these consequences of anger has also been studied as a possible contributor in the development of hypertension and coronary heart disease (Robins & Novaco, 2000.)

What I find intriguing and yet explainable is that the medical conditions most commonly connected with major depression were Fibromyalgia and Chronic Fatigue syndrome (Patten, Beck, Kassam, Williams, Barbui, & Metz, 2005). As a result of the frequency of depression in those with either of these disorders, there has been a conclusion drawn that depression is a secondary component of each of these conditions. I disagree. I believe that depression is neither a primary nor a secondary component of either. This psychological response may quite possibly have nothing at all to do with the disorders themselves but with the prognosis given to those who have either Fibromyalgia or chronic fatigue. These patients are often told that they have a chronic degenerative disorder and pain that may never end.

For those who are prone to giving their power away to others, this life sentence could naturally result in depression and hopelessness. As a result of my work over the years with clients presenting with both psychological and physical difficulties, I have come to believe strongly that the degree of depression corresponds completely with the extent to which you believe you are powerless. If we want to eliminate depression, we need to look at where the belief in powerlessness comes from and why it is being sustained.Although this chapter is about Fibromyalgia research, I would like to present just one case of Chronic Fatigue syndrome that I worked with since many factors in this case are similar to those in multiple cases, and the story says it all.

A very weak-looking young woman of about 25 came into my office using a walker. Behind her was a very good-looking man who helped her in every way he could and with such a loving smile. When we were alone, I asked if that was her boyfriend and she said no. He had been her fiancé but they had broken up as a result of her prognosis. Her ex-fiancé wanted children and the doctor had told her that having children could seriously harm, if not kill, this young woman. She did not want to deprive her fiancé of his dream so she broke up with him. Clearly, he had not gone far.... Combining the energy work with therapy, we were able to help her gain some mobility and fluidity back into her legs, as well as begin to bring her passion and immune function up to a more reasonable level.

After a few sessions, while she was on the table, I had a vision of her standing in a fenced-in playground surrounded by children of varying heights and ages. Since she used a wheel-chair at home and a walker when she went out, I asked her what she did all day, just to open up a possible discussion. She told me she read and spent a lot of time on her computer, which was where she had found me. She had been the first person in her family ever to go to college. Her parents, who were from the "old country," were blue collar workers and had each worked two jobs to put her through school.

They felt that a good girl in America became a teacher, and so she fulfilled their dream. They now, however, were devastated while watching their daughter disintegrating before their eyes. I asked her how she had liked teaching and she stated that she hated it. She taught the first year she was out of college and convinced herself that the reason she didn't like it was because it was new and she felt insecure. She dreaded going back the following September and with each month that passed, she felt progressively more exhausted and disheartened at needing to have this position, yet she forced herself out of bed to teach each morning. By the winter break she could no longer go to school. Shortly after that she got the diagnosis of Chronic Fatigue Syndrome, supposedly a chronic, debilitating disorder.

When I asked what she would do if she could do anything in this world, she told me she would love to work with children but in sports - she would love to be a gym instructor. I asked if there was a Boys and Girls Club in her area and she said there was one just up the street from her parents' home. I suggested she ask if she could volunteer two mornings a week if she had the strength, just to get out of the house. She did just that and after a period of time she was asked to work, for pay, two full days a week. She continued to see me weekly and was now walking with a cane her parents had excitedly bought for her. Eventually, she was able to work full-time at this facility, became sports director, and then married her fiancé. I saw her once a month for a period of time while she was pregnant with her first child.

This young woman was no longer chronically tired of her life and where it was going, but was now filled with passion, vibrancy, and a very strong faith. Depression was no longer a part of her life and neither was her chronic, degenerative disorder. You can heal yourself if you are willing to remember who you are and listen to what your heart and soul are telling you. Her parents were not devastated at their daughter's job change; they were overwhelmed with her recovery and with becoming grandparents. Serious disorders require serious change and the difficulty is that many of you do not know what change would be required or if you are even able to accomplish such a feat.

In looking at how this relates to Fibromyalgia, it appears to be quite possible that the presence of depression, although not an aspect of Fibromyalgia itself, could also inhibit the ability for Fibromyalgia patients to heal. Depression inhibits the ability for full emotional expression, a natural way to have our body's energy flowing freely, and instead supports the stagnant, stuck energy of Fibromyalgia. In view of that fact, medical personnel need to understand the necessity of presenting what is, rather than to projecting a limited future, when what we are seeing, even if with anecdotal research at the moment, is that a patient's beliefs and emotional state impact his or her prognosis immensely, perhaps even more than the disorder or disease itself.

For many I meet, it seems as if the light has gone out. There is a survival existence, yet the passion, vibrancy, and aliveness that make you giggle, laugh, and thoroughly enjoy the fun of the journey are missing. When I am asked often why I am so "up" all the time or why my outlook is so different from that of others, my only response is that life is a really fun adventure. We all have difficulties, we all get in our own way, and we are all searching at times, yet the trip can be such a joy if we can keep things in perspective. Think of where you were in your life at 18. Didn't you have visions of what it was all going to look like? Does any of it look as you anticipated? You can be disappointed or in awe. If you can, own that your life is what you made it, and if you don't like it, you can change it...

For me, knowing that there is so much more to this world than what we see with our eyes, permits me to put things in a perspective that offers me the outlook that there is always so much going on if I want to participate. It is life-giving. I also know that when I need alone time, I can crawl into the tub and take a nurturing Epson salt bath, go to a movie, or read a book. Think of what having those options, if you choose them, can do for your physical body versus feeling powerless and being depressed.

The curiosity, expansiveness, exuberance, and joy of those of you who are consciously attempting to walk a path of spiritual purpose can be so dramatically different from that of those who are merely surviving or living without a greater sense of purpose. By working in the field of body-centered psychotherapy for over twenty years, I have seen first-hand the impact of a positive and life-supporting belief system demonstrated again and again by clients who have overcome odds that would have caused others to give up. The power of the mind and of faith is unlimited. Miracles can happen daily when you allow them and when you expect them.

Including spirituality as a component of a physical disorder in this research was done to provide scientific exploration into the expansion of mind/body medicine. Specifically, this research was, for me, a means of possibly providing insight into the development of disease and disorders. Questions that were considered included: Does a lack of health begin solely on the physical level? On the emotional level? The intellectual level? Or is the beginning of all illness actually on the spiritual level?

In collecting anecdotal data through much of my practice, I noticed that people with certain disorders seemed to have similar psycho/spiritual traits, to such an extent that even, with cancer, which has many forms, the various types of cancer seem to be more common in specific personality constructs. In this research, I wanted to see if that theory regarding the connection between specific disorders and certain psycho-spiritual traits would prove to be true or if it were simply a hypothesis that could not be supported.

I had noticed that with Fibromyalgia, there was a common theme as well. Every one of us may define the word "love" differently since it means different things to different people, depending upon childhood and adult-life experiences. For those with Fibromyalgia, the common theme that I saw was that love means to protect. Spiritually, it seems that many with this disorder believe that their spiritual purpose on this journey is to protect those they love from possible harm, fear, failure, loneliness, and sadness or depression. If they were to fail, they believe they would be failing themselves, as well as those they love.

Most parents want to protect their child and most want to protect a loved one, yet it is the extreme example of that desire to protect those loved ones that predisposes someone to this disorder. One client in Connecticut had a child getting married and moving to California; another had a child going to college in Colorado. One woman who had recently placed her mother in a nursing home realized, after taking a weekend away, that she was consumed with fear for her mother. She resented the fact that she did not have children since she did not want excessive responsibility, and yet the entire weekend she was away she felt like a mother since she feared that her mother would not get her medications as needed, may miss a meal, or might fall out of bed and not be found quickly. For her, this felt too much like having a child she was too frightened to leave. This was nothing that she wanted in her life and she has recently started having a great deal of physical pain.

In order to get a full picture of the condition of Fibromyalgia and be able to assess the validity of my observations that there may be specific emotional and spiritual components to this disorder, I initially did the quantitative scientific research supported by the NIH grant funding. After the completion of that project, using a sampling of the participants who had completed that portion of the research, from the control and treatment groups equally, I did qualitative research to be able to better understand their experience of the disorder, and their life story before and after diagnosis.

Before beginning the research, I reviewed previous studies. One stated that Fibromyalgia is associated with panic disorder and functional dyspepsia with mood disorders (Arnold, 2000), while another associated Fibromyalgia with a tendency of feeling distressed with little sense of coherency (Jamison, 1999). Due to the high levels of stress that can exist in those diagnosed with Fibromyalgia, under conditions of extreme stress, panic attacks, and a possibly resultant lack of coherency would appear to be not too surprising.

In diagnosing Fibromyalgia, physicians press 18 points on the body, most of which are on or near the bladder meridian. If 16 or more are described as "very painful," this diagnosis is given. To understand the role any psychosocial factors may play in emotional responses, looking at childhood conditioning and the resultant character structures can offer some insight as to why we respond or react the way we do.

In regard to Fibromyalgia patients, conditioned responses to over-responsibility as a young child, unless dealt with, predispose them to the experience of not only being overwhelmed as an adult, but also feeling the need to protect current loved ones from being overwhelmed as well by a perceived enemy or difficult situation. The emotional state of a patient who still lives in the reactionary mind-set of such a difficult childhood could be marked by a tendency to overreact, while, understandably, having a pattern of feeling insecure in their attachment to others.

Consequently, enmeshment, or codependency, is not an uncommon pattern in relationship for those with this childhood history, nor is the opposite possibility, at the other end of the spectrum, having great difficulty in forming any type of attachment. These insecure attachment styles were said to be overrepresented in the Fibromyalgia population (Hallberg & Carlsson, 1998; Maunder & Hunter, 2001).

The primary connection between enmeshment versus intimacy and health that was drawn by these researchers was based on a correlation between unmitigated communion and self-neglect. Self-neglect was shown to have a correlation to medical ill health, especially for those with Fibromyalgia, due to their lack of self-care.

My experience with patients with Fibromyalgia is that they tend to be individuals who will put the emotional, physical, and spiritual needs of everyone with whom they are in relationship ahead of their own, to an extreme degree. The patient with Fibromyalgia will, when the pain of Fibromyalgia develops, push forward in spite of it in the attempt to fulfill the needs of the other, whether real or imagined.

Quantitative Research:

What follows is a listing of the tools used in the research and the formatting used:

1. The Pain Intensity Scale and The Pain Attention Scale: With Fibromyalgia patients, pain varies in intensity and location. Using the method of Affleck, Urrows, Tennen, Higgins, and Abeles (1996), my research team updated the participant's pain intensity at the time of the initial interview in each of 18 areas of the body: neck, shoulders, chest, buttocks, upper and lower back, right and left upper arm, right and left lower arm, right and left upper leg, right and left lower leg. Pain intensity was scored on a 0-6 scale: 0 = none, 2 = mild, 4 = moderate, and 6 = severe. We had the participant rate how much his or her attention had been focused on their pain during the last 30 minutes. The scale was 0-6, with 0 = none and 6 = extremely.
2. The Fibromyalgia Impact Questionnaire: This questionnaire is composed of 10 items. The first item has 11 questions relating to physical functioning. Items 2 and 3 ask for the number of days a patient felt well or was unable to work. Additional questions relate to pain, fatigue, stiffness, anxiety, and depression. Early assessments have demonstrated that the FIQ has sufficient evidence of reliability and validity to warrant further testing in both research and clinical settings (Burckhardt, Clark, & Bennett, 1991).
3. The Pain Catastrophizing Scale is a validated questionnaire that asks Fibromyalgia participants to indicate the extent to which they have experienced each of 13 thoughts or feelings when experiencing pain. The ratings are done using a 5 point scale where 0 = not at all and 4 =all the time. This scale was marked by each participant based on the individual's previous week's experience. (Sullivan, 1995)
4. The Unmitigated Communion Scale is a scale used to estimate a person's tendency to focus on others to the exclusion of the self. One hypothesis I tested was that persons who present with Fibromyalgia have a tendency to overprotect another person.

This scale asks the participant to respond to 9 specific statements using a Likert scale from 1 - 5 (strongly agree to strongly disagree) (Fritz & Helgeson, 1998).

The reasons they were chosen are:

- The Unmitigated Communion Scale:
  The use of the Unmitigated Communion Scale was intended to measure whether and to what extent Fibromyalgia patients were over-involved or had a loss of self in relationship. A more in-depth assessment found in the qualitative research provides an understanding of these conditions as being a result of many participants' inability to set boundaries; to confront difficult situations, due to a fear of hurting others; or to express their needs, due to a fear of imposing, or being "high maintenance." Finally, some results conclude that an "unprotected self" that developed as a result of unsafe conditions in childhood, impacted adult psychological functioning and was mirrored in Fibromyalgia, along with a hypomanic helplessness (Wentz, Lindberg, & Hallberg, 2004).
- The Pain Catastrophizing Questionnaire: This questionnaire was included to determine the level to which those with Fibromyalgia over-react to stimuli. Because of an intrinsically high fear level, any stimuli can generate an over-reaction.
- The Pain Attention Scale: This scale was included because of a tendency of such patients to focus on the pain that occurred yesterday, that pain that may occur today, and the pain that will probably occur tomorrow. An excessive amount of attention is paid to the pain to the extent that it begins to define the patient. Everything about them becomes defined by the pain.
- The Pain Intensity Scale: This scale was chosen because of an inclination of those involved to measure their life experience by the level of pain intensity.
- The Fibromyalgia Impact Questionnaire:
  This questionnaire provides an accurate reading of the participants' ability to function in their day to day life.

Prior to the 1st, 4th, 8th, and 12th weeks' sessions, the participants completed these questionnaires and scales. After the first week's questionnaires and scales were completed, the participant was assigned by randomized computer selection to either the treatment or the control group. This approach to the study involved the recruitment of 50 participants to explore the possibility of any consistent psycho/spiritual correlation among participants.

The intention was to have 25 participants in each of the control and treatment groups. The difficulty that occurred shortly into the recruitment was that, due to the lack of a traditional control group, some of those placed in the controls were immediately aware of their selection to that group and chose not to participate.

The energy healing group received eight weekly treatment sessions of the W.I.S.E.™ Method (discussed below) for 45 minutes. The relaxation group received eight weekly relaxation sessions with a slightly different routine. For the relaxation group, the first 15 minutes of each session was spent with a research staff member and was social in nature to ensure each group had human contact, while the remaining half hour was simply a relaxation session (using audiotape) with the staff member present.

At the 12-week point, a follow-up visit to assess the tendency to maintain, improve, or regress occurred. Control group members received a treatment session during this visit, if desired, as a token of thanks for completion of participation. In addition, each participant in both the control and treatments groups self-reported before and after each session on pain, stress, and outlook, rating 1-10 using the Likert Scale.

The W.I.S.E.™ Method:

The W.I.S.E.™ Method (Wholistic, Integrated, Spiritual, Energy) which I developed, is the method of Energy Medicine used in this research. I had previously pursued certification in acupressure, reflexology, iridology, Jin Shin Do, Barbara Brennan Healing Science, hypnotherapy, Reiki, Consegrity, and Breath Work. In combining what I considered to be the best of each of these methods with my knowledge, experience, and training as a licensed clinician in psychotherapy, I developed the basics of The W.I.S.E.™ Method utilizing the tools of both Energy Medicine and Energy Psychology. There are those approaches to Energy Medicine that deal solely with balancing the field; however, this approach includes the premise of Energy Psychology which recognizes that energetic bodies impact, and are impacted by, the personal emotional and spiritual beliefs, and that by shifting energetic patterns we can shift our hold on specific thoughts and beliefs.

To best support the educational and transformational purposes of this method, the practitioner, and, most importantly, the patients, need to become aware of what was going on at the point of onset, or at least at the point of an exacerbation, of the presented disorder or disease. In that way, there is a greater opportunity for patients to recognize their physical reaction to the psycho/spiritual stimuli that might be associated with that pain. In acknowledging the connection, the patient is better able to experience the need for, and benefit of, a reconditioned response.

This very personal approach to wholistic health utilizes energy healing to balance each level of existence with the other, and also supports clients in understanding many of the possible "whys" of any disorder, disease, or accident, as well as empowering and enlightening them to work more fully with whatever symptoms are impacting their lives.

Both the quantitative and qualitative approaches to this proposed research addressed these specific research questions:

1. Does Energy Psychology, specifically as used within the W.I.S.E.™ Method, have an effect on pain, on physical function, or on the quality of life in patients with Fibromyalgia?
2. Is the effect of the W.I.S.E.™ Method greater than, equal to, or less than that of the usual allopathic treatment coupled with a relaxation session?
3. Are there specific psycho/spiritual beliefs that predispose a patient to the development of this specific disorder? If so, in Fibromyalgia, are those belief systems related to a possible tendency to overprotect those individuals the patient is in relationship with from life itself, including any possible negative consequences of the life choices the child/partner/parent or friend may make?

> For purposes of this study, overprotection is perceived to occur at the point where the individual who is loved does not have the freedom to make a mistake, to fail, to fall, or to choose for him- or herself due to extensive over-involvement or control by the caretaker

In observing the results of the data presented on the scales below, we get a picture of the results of the quantitative aspect of the research solely in regard to the specific tools that were used by the project manager for data collection, including again, the Fibromyalgia Impact Questionnaire, the Pain Intensity Scale, Pain Attention Scale, PainCatastrophizing Scale, and the Unmitigated Communion Scale. The first scale to be discussed:

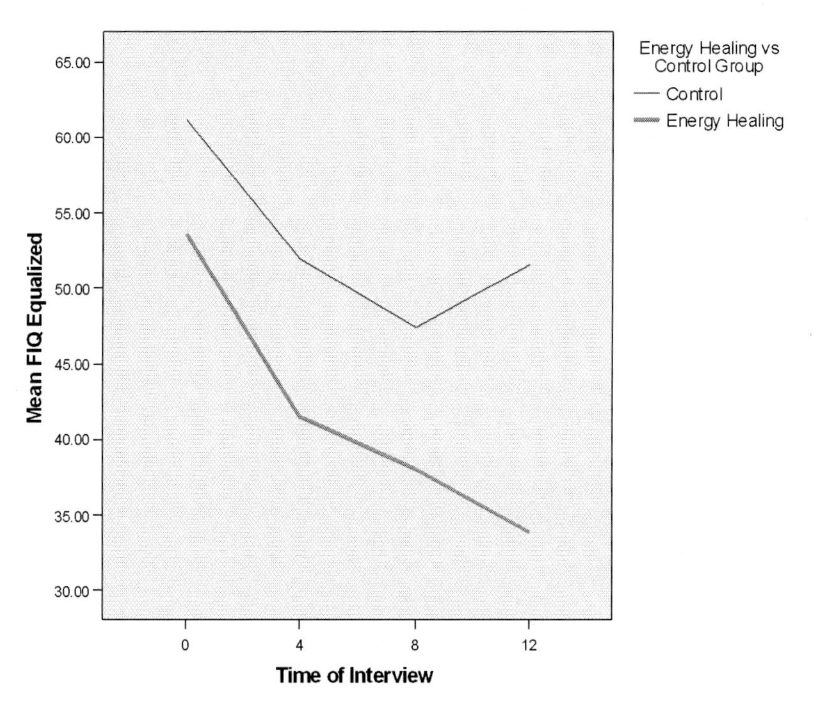

Figure 1. Fibromyalgia Impact Questionnaire

This questionnaire assesses the impact of Fibromyalgia on the day to day life of the participant. It contains questions regarding such issues as the ability for shopping, doing laundry, preparing meals, and driving. In addition, it covers difficulties such as tiredness, pain, stiffness, nervousness, and depression. The lines indicate the extent to which physical limitations impact the participants, while the numbers on the bottom indicate the number of weeks into the research at the time the questionnaire was administered.

The most significant difference between the treatment and control groups is to be noted in the ability of the treatment group to continue improvements during the four-week period between the end of the treatment sessions and the call-back to assess the ability for maintenance or improvement, while allowing also for possible regression to an earlier state of health and function for the participant. Because the treatment group was instructed in techniques for recognizing possible catalysts for an exacerbation, they were also taught tools for relaxation and for reframing of the stimuli to support a less dramatic and short-lived physical effect, if any at all.

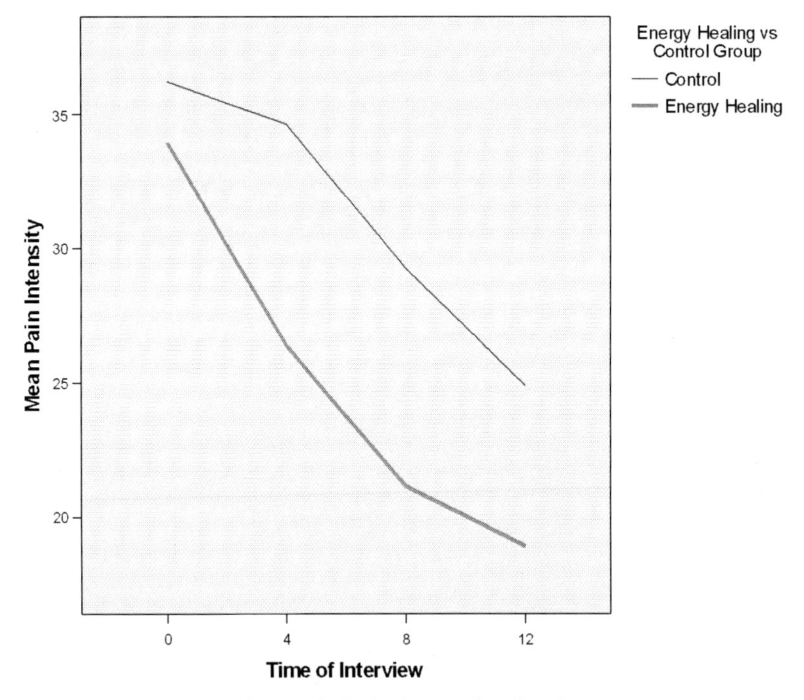

Figure 2. Pain Intensity Scale

As with the Fibromyalgia Impact Questionnaire, there is considerable improvement in pain intensity shown in the results for the Pain Intensity instrument. In this instance, although the treatment group fares better from the beginning of the process and throughout, as is the norm in this series of tools, there is continuous improvement for each group.

One question to ask, for both groups, is whether the improvement was impacted simply by having the ability, or permission, to take time for the self to relax, allow for focus on the self, and do self-care. Was the opportunity and ability for relaxation, in either group, sufficient to support the body in having the opportunity to heal, to let go, and to remember the experience of calm, however relative that may have been?

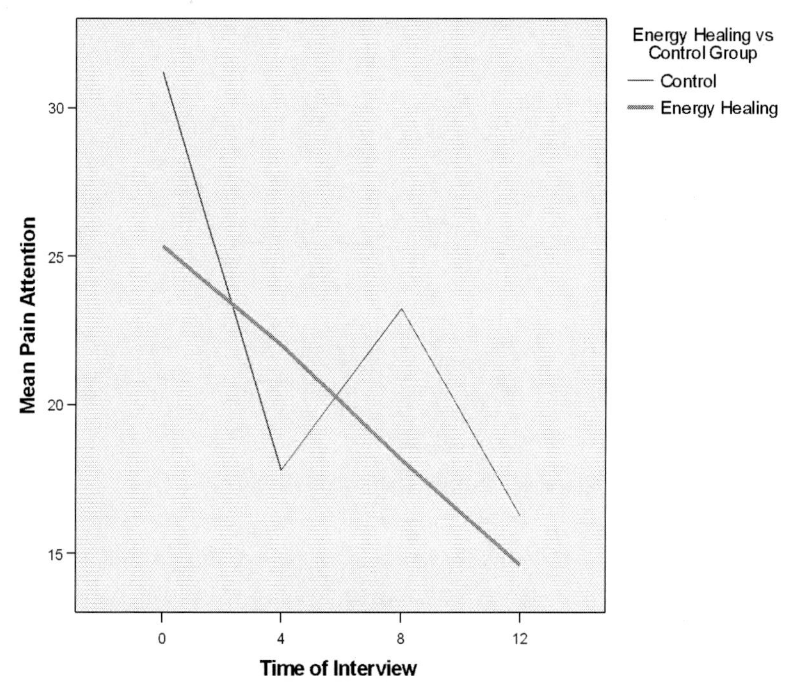

Figure 3. Pain Attention Scale

This table demonstrates the amount of times each participant paid attention to the pain s/he had at the moment, as well as the amount of time s/he spent living in the memory of the pain, or, finally, how frequently s/he lived in anticipation of when the pain would come again and what that would entail.

Although there is a difference shown in the comparison of the treatment and control groups, both ended fairly close to the other. There clearly was a more consistent improvement in the treatment group, with a higher end point, although, overall, the control group made a greater degree of shift from beginning to end.

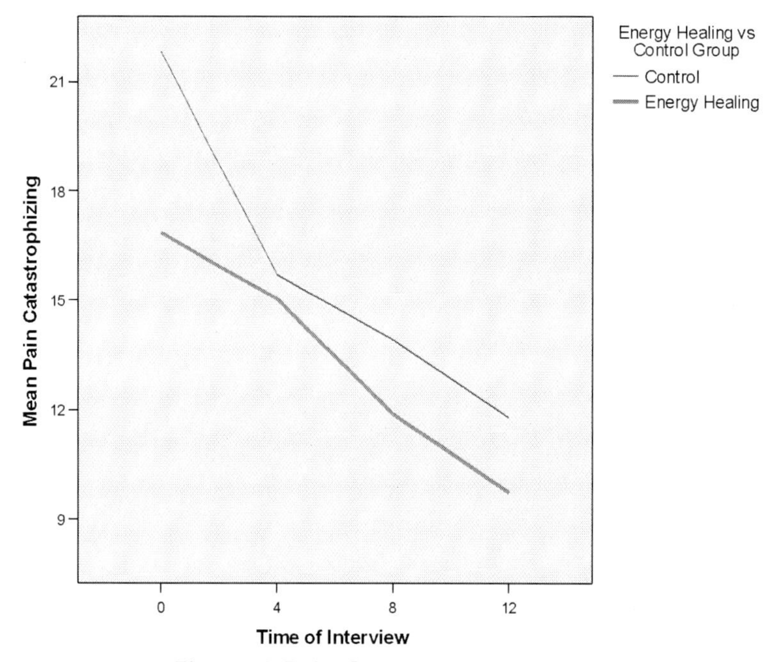

Figure 4. Pain Catastrophizing Scale

It is accepted by practitioners working with the Fibromyalgia population that there is a tendency to exaggerate, or catastrophize, the level of pain experienced. This was measured in occurrences as reported by the participants. One possible cause of this may be the secondary disorders of depression and tiredness that are common in Fibromyalgia patients. The control group had more pain catastrophizing to begin with, and ended with more as well. For the control group, week 4 demonstrated a change in the patterning in pain intensity, pain attention, and, finally, in pain catastrophizing.

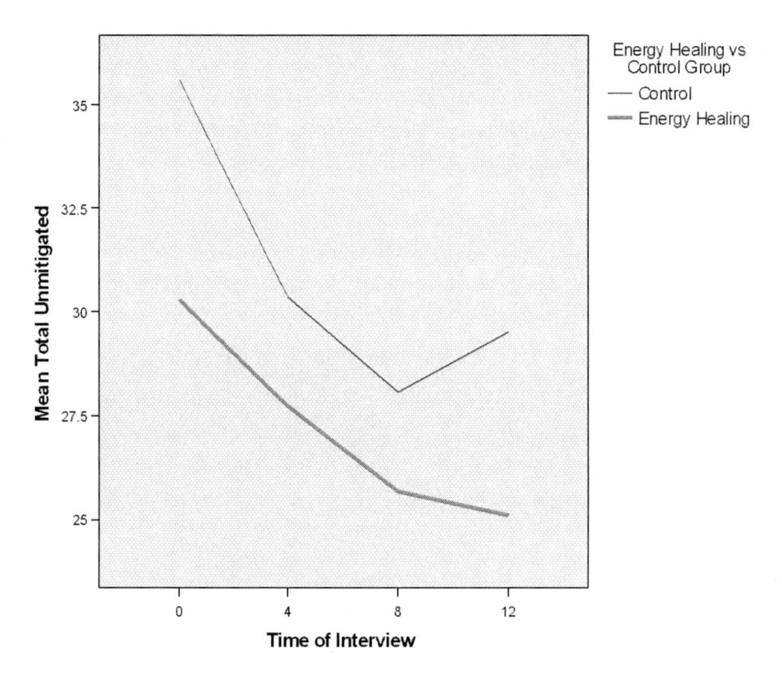

Figure 5. Unmitigated Communion Scale

The Unmitigated Communion Scale was used in this research project due to the premise that the personality style of a Fibromyalgia patient is one of an individual who has a tendency to be over-invested, enmeshed, and codependent in relationships. The questions asked gave a clear indication of the patterns in the relationships of the participants. A key factor can be observed in that, although improvement had been steady in each group for the first 8 weeks, at the point of the 8th week, when the participants were on their own for the next 4 weeks, there is a sharp twist away from improvement in the control group.

Once the relaxation sessions, during which the participants were the center of attention by the practitioners for 45-50 minutes each week, had stopped, these individuals began the regression back to the older pattern of focusing on another.

One difference in the treatment group is that there was specific direction to look at behavior patterns in relationships, recognizing the need to say no, to differentiate the needs of the other from the needs of self, and to recognize the physiological change that took place when this occurred. This is a simple skill set to teach, and yet a difficult one for a participant to accept without guilt or confusion. Once accepted and implemented by the study group, however, clear differences in healing can be seen between the groups.

In addition to completing the questionnaires above, which were completed just prior to the 1st, 4th, 8th, and 12th week sessions, the participants were also asked each week, prior to listening to the tape or receiving treatment, to assess their pain, stress, and outlook levels for the week. They were questioned again upon completion of each session.

This desire for additional weekly information was based on a need to see more specific periods of change, if any, that each patient achieved in shorter and more specific timespans. The tables were set to range from a choice of 1–10, with 1 being minimal pain, and 10 being most severe. In review, the energy treatment group received a 45-50 minute energy therapy treatment each week for 8 weeks from a graduate of a 4-year energy therapy training program, with a final session at the 12th week point.

The control group was greeted by a 1st year student who had a minimal amount of exposure to and/or understanding of energy therapy. After an initial greeting, the participant was asked to get comfortable, lying or sitting, and to listen to a relaxation tape for almost 45 minutes, with the student staying in the room. As with the treatment group, there were 8 weekly sessions, with a final session in the 12th week to assess maintenance, improvement, or regression in sustaining any improvements that may have taken place.

The most obvious point of notice within this table is the percentage of drop-outs amongst the control group, 47.05%, versus 7.7% for the treatment group. Another point of interest is the final readings. In the tables below are the percentages, first in conjunction with all assigned participants to each group, and second in comparison only to those who had completed the research.

Table 1
Placement of Final Reading Scores—Total Group

Final Readings	**Treatment**	**Control**
Total Number in Group	26	17
All 1s*	65.38%	11.76%
Reading scores from 2-4	15.38%	17.64%
Reading scores from 5-10	11.50%	23.53%

* 1 = least amount of pain

The percentage of participants capable of attaining a score of all 1s tends towards a noticeable difference between the treatment and control groups in favor of the treatment group.

The differences between groups in percentage of those whose readings were from 5-10 are clearly notable, as well, although the percentages are lower.

In comparing Tables 1 and 2, the percentage difference between the groups of those who completed the research versus those who did not appear excessive. For those who completed, the treatment group exceeds the control group, demonstrating a clear message of the impact of Energy Medicine, or energy therapy, versus relaxation tapes.

Table 2
Placement of Final Reading Scores: Those Who Completed

Final Readings	**Treatment**	**Control**
Members who completed research	24	9
All 1s*	70.83%	22.22%
Reading scores from 2-4	16.66%	33.33%
Reading scores from 5-10	12.50%	44.44%

* 1-least amount of pain

Percentage-wise, certainly the treatment group did better in all cases, yet, for the treatment group itself, in comparing both total and completed tallies, there is not a great difference between the readings.

However, for the control group, in comparing both total and completed tallies, the differences are almost doubled for each line item. This again confirms the need for retention of participants to ensure at least an opportunity for greater parity.

An additional figure in assessing the impact of the sessions is calculated by noting the changes that have taken place from the first to the last readings. These are shown in the table below.

Table 3
Percentage of Change Between First and Last Session

	Treatment	**Control**
Total Completed	24	9
Improved		
1-5 points	5 = 20.8%	2 = 22.2%
6-9 points	8 = 33.3%	2 = 22.2%
10-15 points	10 = 41.6%	1 = 11.1%
16 -20 points		2 = 22.2%
Regressed		
1-5 points		1 = 11.1%
6-9 points	1 = 4.2%	
10-15 points		
Remained the Same		1 = 11.1%

It is significant to note the differences not just between groups, but what changes were possible for the participants themselves between the first and last sessions. What best supported them? For a disorder that has been classified as a chronic debilitating disorder, our results demonstrate that the prognosis is not always correct.

The participants in the treatment group who completed the process were able to achieve a level of function and mobility that far surpassed what they had had in recent years, despite possible prognoses to the contrary. There is hope that more can be done, with more time. Table 3 shows this ability for dramatic change.

General Conclusions from the Scales

Through results obtained with these scales, it is evident that functionality and pain intensity can be changed with Energy Medicine, far more so than with simple relaxation techniques. Clearly, the physical level is far easier to change, and to change significantly, even within 8 weeks. As a result, for the first 8 weeks, each group consistently showed improvement, even though the treatment group was stronger in its recovery.

This provides evidence that the physical can shift fairly rapidly with attention and care, especially when we consider that some of these patients had been diagnosed for 10 or more years. With education and a potentially resultant change in behavior, the treatment group may have developed the ability to recognize immediately any pain that developed, while also having the ability to quickly release it.

The control group might have become accustomed to receiving care and might have returned to treatment as needed, thus supporting a higher level of functioning than was previously achieved without the relaxation process. Throughout all of these tests, it was clear from comments the participants made, that they "knew" they were not "listening" to themselves; they knew "inside" what they should do yet felt immensely responsible for the others in their lives to the extent that they ignored what they "knew."

The last three scales, Pain Attention, Pain Catastrophizing, and the Unmitigated Communion Scale, are all impacted by the psycho/spiritual development of each patient, rather than solely measuring physical shifts. Although improvement was displayed in each of these scales, for significant shifts to take place in regard to the specific scales that focus on the inner psychodynamics of the individual's relationship to self, as well as on his or her relationship to the other, it is clear from these scales that a longer period of intervention may be necessary.

Each of these particular scales relates to the world view of the patient. In pain attention, it is the victim mentality, seeing life as a struggle or an uphill climb, that keeps him or her living from a perspective of going from pain episode to pain episode, while being governed by these pain episodes. Life from that perspective is clearly about pain. I would suspect that pain was a part of their life, emotionally or spiritually, long before their experience with Fibromyalgia.

The Pain Attention Scale registers the degree to which the patient currently focuses on the pain of the past, any possible pain of the present, and the anticipated pain of the future. To change that emphasis, or to learn to keep things in perspective with whatever else is going on in life, takes practice. As more research, anecdotal or empirical, takes place within Energy Psychology and Energy Medicine, other approaches may prove to be more successful, not only in the immediate future but in the long-term as well, not only with Fibromyalgia but also with other disorders.

Pain Catastrophizing is characteristic of individuals who focused on their pain, while also traumatizing their experience. For many of these individuals, their disorder and their pain is their sense of identity. For some, their Fibromyalgia support group is their only socialization. To be without pain, to be healed, could mean a loss of their only social activities and their only friends. The price of healing could be too high, and the need for pain, even significant pain, as an identification tool is a necessary point of their belonging.

As a result, far more than 8 weeks is needed for most patients to support a reframing of their life, their illness, and their role in the larger picture. Many of the patients in this research had never been in psychotherapy and saw no need for it. Consequently, changing their world view, if they were willing, would require, as became evident in this research, far longer than the 8-week time period allocated in this pilot study.

The Unmitigated Communion Scale reflected the emotional and physical dependency patterns of those with Fibromyalgia. The difficulty in working directly with the emotional level of behavior is demonstrated in the Unmitigated Communion Scale, the one scale solely reflecting emotional change, rising only from 25-35. Psychodynamics can be impacted by Energy Medicine or Energy Psychology and in using this inclusive approach, but it appears that the specific psychodynamic changes needed must be reiterated on a conscious level if the change is to be sustained and progressive.

Seeing oneself as a victim, or as powerless, supports continued imbalance and self-negation factors that need to be addressed in order to understand the multileveled impact from such a belief. The enmeshment patterns of relationship, from the perspective of these participants—in which they perceive themselves as having no real significance other than for service—make it difficult realistically to expect them to balance service with self-care and personal development at all. To expect them to do so in 8 weeks is clearly unrealistic. This is one aspect of the findings that is not a surprise, and yet, at the same time, was not anticipated.

As we go further into the world of energy research, in whatever form, we need to assess both the long-term and short-term impact of this work. It is usually fairly easy to make an immediate change in someone's health with Energy Medicine. The client's ability to sustain that change, or even to improve upon it, defines the true effectiveness of the multi-dimensional shift and needs to be a part of the overall assessment of a method's effectiveness. We were blessed to see some of our participants from the treatment group a year later, and they were still without pain after a previous 10-15 years of being limited due to their Fibromyalgia. Learning to listen and having permission for self-care were two of the major lessons that were carried throughout this project.

CHAPTER EIGHTEEN

Qualitative Research in Energy Medicine and Energy Psychology

The Qualitative Research

The qualitative component of this research design consisted of one-hour in-depth interviews in a semi-structured format and provided the opportunity to conduct more extensive, personal, and in-depth research. The 12 interviewees, 6 each from the control and treatment groups, had completed their participation in the original quantitative process of this study. Based on the recommendation of John Creswell (1998), in which he states that a total number of 10 participants is recommended in phenomenological studies, I chose to involve 12 participants to provide additional support to the validity of the findings.

Specific questions were asked, but in no defined order. Some were answered without being asked. The participant was permitted to lead the interview in any way he or she desired, discussing any additional points or stories he or she chose to present. The questions were asked when it seemed appropriate to the topic being discussed.

Listed below are the questions asked in the interview process:

- How do you see your role, or purpose, in life as it is now?
- Has that view changed?
- What are your expectations of the people you are in relationship with?

- Have they changed?
- Do you need permission from you and others to pursue your dreams?
- Do you have the time or desire to pursue them?
- What are they?
- Do you have a spiritual practice? What does that mean for you?
- Now that the sessions have ended, have the physical problems remained?
- Have they increased or lessened? If so, in what way?
- If you have one, how has your support system sustained you in dealing with chronic pain? Any changes?
- How has that impacted your view of the world and those in it?
- How has that impacted your role in this world of yours?
- Do you relate any of the above to the sessions received?
- To the practitioner you worked with?

Due to the volume of the data collected, I will only provide a sampling of the questions and answers. Some of the additional information given during the course of the interviews follows the responses to the specific questions asked. Where necessary, a summary of a long response has been used to support the general meaning or flavor of the interview. What I observed in this aspect of the research was that the need to give and support was most definitely a theme among the participants.

It had been demonstrated, during the quantitative research phase, that there were a few women who wanted to participate fully in order to feel better, yet who felt compelled to leave early so that their husband's dinner would be on the table on time since "he gets angry if he needs to wait." The stress in their bodies would be rekindled shortly after they mentioned how much better they felt during a session. With the stress level increasing, it is important to note that the tendency to focus on the "other" blocked the ability to lie in the silence, listening to what their body/soul had to say about their recovery, rather than fearing what their husband would say about a meal being 10 - 15 minutes late, or perhaps conceiving of the idea of him serving himself.

To support confidentiality, fictitious names were developed:

1. Alice	7. Gerry
2. Barbara	8. Helen
3. Carol	9. Iris
4. Diane	10. Jack
5. Edna	11. Karen
6. Frances	12. Linda

How do you see your role in life as it is now?

1. "I don't know, as taking care of everyone in my life."
2. "I am now evolving."
3. "Every day I need to try to become a better healer for others."
4. "I wanted to stay home, always. Now I can get to take care of others better."
5. "Now, I don't know, I was forced to retire because of fibro and lost money."
6. "Retiring. Now dealing with issues I never had time to deal with before."
7. "I don't know if I have a purpose; it is more that I need to find joy in life."
8. "I like my life now. I take care of people when I want."
9. "I live for my family, my husband, mother, daughter, and aunt. I'm busy."
10. "I still have things to offer. Who I am in the world and what I want to give to the world changes constantly. I want to support people and to lovingly give more."
11. "I don't know."
12. "I am a giver. A very caring person and I see myself taking care of others."

This was a question that caused each one, in the private session, to stop the conversation to think. It was as if life had been clearly defined in the past and now there were options. For Alice (1), Carol (3), Diane (4), Helen (8), Iris (9), Jack (10), and Linda (12), it still entailed taking care of others.

Barbara (2) demonstrated a sense of hope that she could become more than she was, although she was in a place of confusion as to how it was that she wanted to evolve. The clearest thought at the moment, even if temporary, was for her to begin an EBay business. It would allow her to focus on what she wanted and what supported her in feeling good about her personal accomplishments. This level of independence, of creating a new life for herself, was a new approach to living and one she was somewhat tentative about, but willing to explore.

Edna (5) carried the theme of "no money and forced retirement" throughout her session. From her perspective, forced retirement and Fibromyalgia took her freedom away. They took her independence. My sense—admittedly an interpretation rather than the usual phenomenological description—was that there was always something that she thought of as taking her freedom away. Fibromyalgia might simply have been the latest item in that list.

Frances (6) referenced issues in relationships and work around the house. Although depressed, Gerry (7) was the only one of the group to mention finding joy in her life. She had no idea how to discover it, but she was going to try. Karen (11) was uncertain of where she belonged right now. Her life is changing and she needs to discover a place for her in it. She feels impeded by a lack of ideas, and by not understanding her options.

Seven participants held a firm belief that service is where they achieve their enjoyment, their sense of purpose, or their worth. For the others, to varying degrees, it was considered an aspect of life, but not necessarily the primary purpose. Barbara, Frances and Jack, who no longer see service as the main purpose of their lives, spoke of the personal growth they have achieved. They now want to find whatever it is that calls them to more enjoyment, feeling more alive, and continuing to evolve.

Although certainly pleasure in giving could exist for the majority of those interviewed, the struggle of balancing the different facets of life was an exhausting role that was always repeating itself. Relationships are about responsibility, caretaking, and, if needed, fighting for those who are loved, whether against institutions or individuals. That protective, responsible energy permeated the responses.

I believe completely in service, as a human responsibility to those with whom we walk this earth, as well as for a sense of belonging and purpose in life. Finding the balance of individual self-care and service of others is a challenge we may all experience at times. This balance supports the healthy aspect of service, while imbalance can result in giving from a place of depletion and resentment—and, ultimately, from a belief in our own martyrdom and victimization—or in not giving at all. Finding that transpersonal balance of giving and receiving is a spiritual and emotional task for many. For those with Fibromyalgia, the imbalance appears to be one in which the extreme of giving is taking place, and, for some, resulting in the self being all but lost. Thankfully, in these responses, it can be seen that various levels of balance and imbalance do exist, thus making it possible, perhaps, for some to move more quickly, or to move further, into the healthier end of the continuum with self-permission.

Expectations of Others:

1. "Very high. Most friends disappoint and let you down though."
2. "I don't have any expectations of anyone."
3. "Getting to know who they are rather than who I want them to be."
4. "None, they will only disappoint."
5. "That they know how loving I am and respect my wishes and wants."
6. "I am not a part of them. I feel like an observer. I am learning that they can't read me. I didn't want to be difficult or high maintenance."
7. "I expect them to seek me for help. They need to expect less of me."
8. "To love me, be honest with me, supportive."
9. "I expect them to be emotionally responsible. Honesty, not perfection, but responsibility."
10. "I expect them to accept me where I am and how I am."
11. "I don't really have any. I still have friends from kindergarten however."
12. "None. I am upset with all my family and friends. It is unfair with all that I do."

Whether they were married or single, the feeling of being alone in this world was common with these participants, whether alone in terms of assuming the responsibility for others or in being called to suffer alone, or simply to be alone and misunderstood. Because of the high expectations and judgments that they place on themselves, it is common with this personality construct to place high expectations on others as well.

It is not uncommon, in spite of all that they do, that these individuals see themselves as inadequate, as not doing enough. They feel guilty about their perceived selfishness and human limitations when they simply need time to stop. Because these expectations and judgments usually carry over to others, there is little room left for the humanity of those with whom they are in relationship.

Do you need permission from others to pursue your dreams?

1. "I don't have goals or dreams. They only give you permission to fail and then embarrass my mother."
2. "No. My dream is to have an EBay business and to organize my house."
3. "My husband, my mother, and my own negation of who I am helped keep me down. My dream is to pull off all the layers that have kept me down and to "get out of life and not return. To get it right."
4. "No. I had a dream once to become a nurse. I did it. I look forward to nothing. No dreams any more. I do not have money (and so) I do not have independence."
5. "No. I just cannot inconvenience them with any. I would take on their unhappiness."
6. "It feels like that."
7. "No just time and money to travel and live in 2 places."
8. "No. I got a BA and I come here."
9. "Support but not permission."
10. "Yes."
11. "No. I meet them all."
12. "No, since it is to make a Christian home for others."

Although the responses are mixed, with Barbara (2), Gerry (7), Helen (8), and Iris (9) having a degree of independence or self-definition, the idea of having a dream, for most, seems beyond their scope. Barbara's dream of an EBay business, Gerry's dream to travel and have two homes, Helen's dream to continue growing, and Iris's dream to reach out and support others, appear to give them something to look forward to, and a way of identifying who they are and what they want in their own lives.

Creating a dream can take energy, energy some feel they have used up already, either due to their limited ability because of Fibromyalgia, or due to the limited number of dreams permitted. For many, however, they are depleted because the little energy they have goes to their responsibilities. The burden and distraction of having a dream causes them to let go of that task while also giving them permission to stay focused on the other.

I personally believe that dreaming, having a vision of our future, or of a goal to achieve, is a natural part of growth and of becoming more of who we are. Dreams are only the beginning of our personal transformations. Our dreams are what call us to grow, to transform, and to reach beyond our present situation. They call us to become the embodied soul we are capable of being. I believe, as well, that our dreams are a way for our soul to call us to what it is we have come here to do, something that may have nothing to do with those in our lives, those who are simply our partners on the journey, but not necessarily an integral part of a specific dream from within.

Do you have the time or desire to pursue them?

1. "NA."
2. "I may."
3. "I don't have permission to follow dreams unless they are wild."
4. "No."
5. "No."
6. "No."
7. "I never had any except to make my house mine and not like the neighbors."

8. "That will come when husband graduates from college."
9. "I give myself permission to have dreams, but not the time to do it. I think it is a core belief that I am not supposed to have my life, because someone else could lose theirs. There never was the permission to be."
10. "I have too much pain."
11. "My husband encourages my painting and that helps me."
12. "I am too physically limited because of the pain."

The responses to this question give the message simply. Only one individual mentioned that she currently has the self-permission needed, and yet she stated that she generally does not have the time. Karen (11), who speaks of being encouraged, also states elsewhere that her husband is an ex-military lawyer with "exacting expectations." Is her inability to find the time a result of her own beliefs or the demands of her husband?

What are your dreams?

1. "To be as unremarkable as possible."
2. "An EBay business."
3. "To get out of life and not return."
4. "None."
5. " Spiritual, holy, adventures – going away, fun of creativity – a new business and to rediscover my passion."
6. "To get to a place where I have no regret or negative thinking."
7. "Travel. To live in two places."
8. "To grow."
9. "Reaching out to find a way to help people find a way to deal with what is inside of themselves and to deal with loss."
10. "To golf and play tennis."
11. "Time to see my grandchildren grow up. I don't really have dreams, but if I did have a dream, it would be to be an artist and to have a garden."
12. "To teach others about Fibromyalgia and this work."

For those who had no permission to dream, or had limited time, there is demonstrated here an almost full list of hopes and dreams presented in response to this question. Some, such as, "To be as unremarkable as possible," or "To get out of life and not return," are certainly not what many would consider a dream of transformation or growth, yet they are dreams. I think of dreams as inspirations. They are something that calls me to reach higher, to have hope, and to play, while enjoying myself and my life. For those who can express their dreams here, what of the previous response wherein they stated that there is no real desire or time to pursue them? Could it be that the dream really does exist, but that what is lacking is permission, whether from themselves or from others to pursue them?

Contradictions can be seen in other areas, as well, when there is a comparison of all the responses provided. It is clear that each individual within this group has his or her own dream, except, of course, for Diane (4), who previously said that she had had a dream to become a nurse, it happened, and now she has no more, and no more desire to create another. Clearly, for most of these individuals, reframing their view of their spiritual purpose, of the reason they exist, and of their right to follow their dreams, is necessary if any of these dreams are to be achieved.

The intent of each of these questions was to provide a larger picture for assessing possible similarities among the participants for observing a possible pattern of psycho/spiritual correlates to a shared physical disorder. In addition, the intent was to assess if particular personality types carry their energy in a particular way, demonstrate physical disorder or disease in a similar way, and have very similar psycho/spiritual beliefs that govern their lives. This knowledge can be utilized in expanding the use of medical treatment, as well as in expanding the content and explanations of the Diagnostic and Statistical Manual of Mental Disorders 4th Ed., (DSM IV - TR).

There are certainly varying degrees of the same issues taking place here. There are various levels of energy being demonstrated by the participants, and yet, their approach to life, to self, to relationships, and to others is all very much in alignment.

If the American Psychological Association (APA) was to approve Energy Psychology as a legitimate approach to mental health, must the

APA first recognize energy as a medical tool? It would also seem that it needs, as well, to see the multi-dimensional impact of energy by recognizing its impact on emotional health, physical and spiritual health as well. The regulating committee may discover that Energy Psychology, from such a perspective, may actually strengthen the field of psychotherapy, rather than weaken it.

Several commonalities were shown during the interviews. My experience of these participants is that they, as a group, are truly caring and supportive individuals. They have an honest desire to support those people they know, and, for some, to support even strangers, in any way they can. The energetic imbalance comes into play in that, rather than that desire being an aspect of their lives or a trait they possess, it becomes their driving force and one that, because it can cause them to lose perspective, can result in an emotional need and responsibility to rescue people who oftentimes do not need or want rescuing. Rather than supporting others as needed, these individuals can come to carry the burden and responsibility of others as their own.

The joy of giving becomes the burden of responsibility. It is at this point, the point of compulsiveness, that a truly loving and supportive characteristic becomes a means of self-betrayal and unhealthy negation. It is here that the cost becomes too high. I would suspect that, in childhood, these individuals were the oldest child, or perhaps the oldest girl, since those positions were usually expected to carry the load in the family, or they rushed in of their own accord to protect and support siblings or the weaker parent, due to parental alcoholism or another limitation in the parents' ability to fulfill their role.

Consequently, from early on in their journey, these individuals learned self-sacrifice for the greater good. It became a pattern of behavior ingrained long before adulthood and adult relationships were considered. For naturally loving, supportive individuals, there needs to be permission to differentiate between taking on unnecessary responsibility for another, and helping others when there is the time and the inclination.

The permission to say "No" is a large step in the integration of self into a relationship. It can provide much needed freedom and the capacity for joy in self-determination. Giving to and comforting others will always be a part of who these individuals are. They are a gift to others, by their nature. Balance is all that is needed, and yet it requires a major shift in world view and a major adjustment to having permission to exist, while believing that this does not take something from another but only adds to the relationship.

Loneliness, perhaps from childhood forward, and possibly the need to protect the others in a way that they were not themselves protected, as well as the desire to be seen as powerful, are fairly consistent throughout, even, I believe, for Alice, who said her dream is basically to be invisible, or "as unremarkable as possible." If the possibility of being seen without needing to serve, or without being hurt, was an option, she might then permit herself the gift of being seen.

Barbara described Fibromyalgia as "a neurological manifestation of a viral agent." Whether that is true or not, there are many aspects to Fibromyalgia that need to be considered in its treatment. It can become one more factor in the life of burdened and overwhelmed individuals who may never have had the freedom to live life as fully as they are capable of doing. For many with this physical disorder, even if improvement were to occur, other illnesses or disorders may continue to present themselves.

CHAPTER NINETEEN

Conclusion

After twenty five years in the field of Energy Medicine, watching all of the changes that have taken place, and the numerous modalities that have developed, I shift between feeling very much like an old timer and feeling as if I am only at the beginning. At one time, there were only a few known modalities with only 3 recognized leaders in the field teaching in this country. The field of Energy Medicine now has practitioners, teachers, and classes throughout the country. That is quite a change.

In order to best incorporate this new dimension of health care, in acknowledging the power of spiritual beliefs and psychology in health, we truly need to develop a new world view, a new way of looking at disease and healing, that permits us to see what we could not acknowledge previously. In understanding the impact of transplant surgery and the realization that the cellular memory of one individual is being physically transferred to another, we need to develop the skills needed to not only support the new technology available but to support those who can benefit from it. They are not simply receiving physical tissue, they are inviting another human being's journey into their body, their cells, and their consciousness, along with all the tastes, preferences, and memories that go with it.

If the Hundredth Monkey Syndrome is to be acknowledged, how far does it apply? If we are now moving more into, or back to, spiritually-based realities of existence and of medicine, are we ready to accept the spiritual reality of the embodied soul within every cell?

A few years ago, while on Anguilla, I received a phone call asking me to assess the difficulty a researcher in Iowa was having in observing aggressive brain cancer cells. Each time the laser moved near the cells, they migrated to the walls of the Petri dish and could not be seen. I suggested she change the energetic environment by using her hands to surround the dish with unconditional love; then, through intention, acknowledge that this is for observation only so that the cells may feel safe and move closer to the center of the dish. Immediately after doing so, the cells all moved to the center and could be observed. All cells crave life and want love, even those in a Petri dish.

In addition, if we are to consider that each disease has its own energetic reality, we need to look at the specialists who work in particular fields. What draws them to that field and what are the potential risks they may be facing if they do not understand the vibration of disease? In discussing this with someone who had been Chief of Staff at a hospital in Arizona, there was a question raised in regard to the high percentage of lung specialists in that hospital that had recently been diagnosed with lung cancer. Should the association of the lungs with grief, along with the emotional connection of other disorders, as Eastern thought teaches, be a necessary part of Western medical training? Would this level of awareness support practitioners in achieving and maintaining their own optimal health especially those in specialized fields where they are immersed in the energy of a particular disease?

What about Energy Medicine practitioners who develop a specialty? Because they are working with the same energetic vibrations consistently, do they need to do their own inner work that relates to their specialty so that they do not begin to have a similar or identical vibration as the disease they are surrounded by hourly?

I was asked to fly to Iowa to work with practitioners who were preparing to do breast cancer research. This group was completing their cervical cancer research during which they worked solely with cervical cancer patients for months. Among the healers, there had been an unusually high rate of cervical cancer that developed during that research even though they did not have the standard markers to be considered prime candidates for the disease. They did not want to risk the possibility of breast cancer development as well and wanted to know how to prepare, multi-dimensionally, for this next research project. Being open to questioning the significance and the impact of working energetically means that we are willing to recognize that there are rewards and costs of which we may not yet be aware.

Understanding the power of psycho/spiritual belief systems and the filters they create will provide another perspective through which disease and disorders can be seen. From this perspective, it is important to note that, clearly, the physical reality needs to be addressed, but not without a context. If wholistic health is to be wholistic, the spirituality, the emotionality, and the physicality of an individual must all be brought into balance and seen as equally significant in a search for health. If food, exercise, laughter, and love are recognized as impacting health, then your spirituality and your psychological frame of reference must also be considered, if the whole person is to be supported.

As you have seen, the whole person includes the embodied soul that calls you to live your life, your journey, in such a way as to continuously become more of who you are meant to be, learning to love yourself and others unconditionally, non-judgmentally, and with all the passion you can permit yourself—to touch from deep within. In forgetting who you are, in negating yourself—or delegating your needs and wants to a place of insignificance, as a way of life—you choose to forget that you are the gift you bring to others in relationship.

What you know, what you do, are simply the additional components of being in relationship with yourself. Until you know what is in your soul, you cannot share the depth of who you are with another and, consequently, you also cannot be fully seen or fully in relationship. It is a lifelong process of unfolding and becoming, and one that requires listening to that voice within.

As I see it, the next step within the fields of psychology, energetic or otherwise, is to recognize the specific psycho/spiritual correlates, or perhaps causes, of specific psychological or physical disorders and disease. These disorders and diseases are the symptoms that allow you to more clearly see the ways in which your vulnerabilities are being expressed and guide you to see how you have lost touch with who you truly are.

This is a new approach to mind/body research, and a new understanding of these energetic bodies and how best to support your health and healing, but one that is needed if you are to support wholistic healing. Providing support in removing the energetic blocks that can exist on each level of healing brings a larger more specific perspective to health on all levels. What a combination of scientific and spiritual approaches that would be.

In *The Web of Life*, Capra discusses a concept known within the chaos theory as the "butterfly effect" that states: "It is a half-joking assertion that a butterfly stirring the air today in Beijing can cause a storm in New York next month" (p. 134). You are living in what appears to be a smaller and smaller world where you can watch events around the globe as they are happening. You are impacted by every catastrophe as well as every great moment that takes place elsewhere.

In becoming global citizens, in recognizing that we all walk together, and that it is our responsibility to support those who have not had the same opportunities, we are compelled to develop our compassion, our empathy, our understanding, and our humor. As we each bring the uniqueness of who we are to the table, not who our trained personalities believe we should be, we are also bringing the world together as one unified and yet individually defined reality.

Supporting the planet, the world community, and our own culture, as well as ourselves, calls us, each one of us, to remember we are here to live, to really live, passionately, vibrantly, and fluidly, bringing out all that we have become to the world, while calling others to do the same.

Our personal and world task then gets filled with all that we are in center stage. Imagine a world where we all speak from the soul, passionately, in joy, and with vibrancy; where we are each free to claim our place on this planet and beyond. We are only beginning this next stage of human and medical evolution.

GLOSSARY

Acupressure – Using finger pressure a practitioner presses or massages defined points in the body that correspond to interior energy flow patterns to adjust blockage, pressure, and flow of the subtle energy bodies.

Acupuncture – Using the same locations as those used in acupressure, very fine needles are inserted to dissipate blockages, balance deficiencies and excesses in flow, and support organic and systemic health.

Barbara Brennan Healing Science – A particular method of Energy Medicine created by Barbara Brennan to balance energy flows within the body on a variety of levels.

Breath Work – Includes several different practitioner methods, all of which use the breath of the body to bring relaxation, balance, and release of blocked energies.

Consegrity – A form of energy balance and healing developed by an orthopedic surgeon, Dr. Mary Lynch, to support the body's own inner wisdom for self- healing, usually through the facilitation of a practitioner.

Defenses – The energetic and personality distortions that we use to protect ourselves from a perceived "enemy" who we believe may want to hurt us physically or emotionally. Their messages of fear distract us from our ability to hear what is being said in the body/soul conversations.

Energy Field – The vibrational energy that surrounds and is within the body.

Energy Psychology – A branch of Energy Medicine with a growing number of techniques using a system of acupressure points to expedite emotional and psychological healing.

Energy Healing – A common term for the balancing and healing of energy blocks, stagnations, or deficiencies within the body to support full-bodied health on the emotional, physical, intellectual, and spiritual levels.

Energy Medicine – A term used to encapsulate the many different approaches developed to support energetic health and healing.

Energy Medicine Practitioner – Can be a global term describing practitioners from a wide variety of modalities of treatment working with the human energy field, although it most commonly refers to those who practice hands-on-healing.

Hundredth Monkey Syndrome – Named by researchers who discovered that after teaching one monkey to wash her vegetables before eating, progressively more were taught - or self taught - until monkeys on neighboring islands had also learned it without guidance.

Hypnotherapy – A technique practiced or taught by a practitioner to support the unconscious in coming forward to be worked with.

Iridology – The study of the eye's iris to assess the health of the body's organs and systems.

Jin Shin Do – A combination of Japanese, Korean, and Chinese acupressure united with American psychiatric thought.

Mask – A pretense we project to others so that we may feel good about who we are.

Psychoneuroimmunology – The study of the interaction between psychological processes and the nervous and immune systems of the human body.

Reflexology – The practice of using finger-point pressure on particular locations, usually on the feet, to create balance throughout the body.

Reiki – Reiki is a Japanese technique for stress reduction and relaxation that also promotes healing.

Subtle Energies – Those energies of the body which are usually perceived only by those with extensive natural gifts or through a high level of training, and which can be manipulated to simultaneously create a healthy, free-flowing body on many levels, including organic and systemic.

REFERENCES

Affleck, G., Urrows, S., Tennen, H., Higgins, P., & Abeles, M. (1996). Sequential daily relations of sleep, pain intensity, and attention to pain among women with fibromyalgia. Pain, 68, 363-368.

Arnold, L. M., Hess, E.V., Hudson, J. L., Welge, J.A., Berno, S. E., & Keck, P. E. (2002). A randomized, placebo-controlled, double-blind, flexible-dose study of fluoxetine in the treatment of women with fibromyalgia. American Journal of Medicine, 112(3), 191-197.

Berkowitz, N., & Martin, H. (2005). The healing power of our past. New York: iUniverse.

Brennan, Barbara Ann. (1988). Hands of light. New York: Bantam.

Burckhardt, C. S., Clark, S. R., & Bebbett, R. M. (1991). The fibromyalgia impact questionnaire: Development and validation. Journal of Rheumatology, 18, 728-734.

Butler, L. D., Koopman, C., Classen, C., & Spiegel, D. (1999). Traumatic events, life stresses, and emotional support in women with metastatic breast cancer: Cancer related traumatic stress symptoms associated with past and current stressors. Health Psychology, 18(6), 555-560.

Capra, Fritjof. (1996). The web of life. New York: Double Day.

Chopra, Deepak. (1999). Foreword. In C. B. Pert, Molecules of emotion: The science behind mind-body medicine. New York: Touchstone.

DeKeyser, Freda. (2003). Psychoneuroimmunology in critically ill patients. AACN Clinical Issues, 14(1), 25-32.

Dossey, Larry. (1993). Healing words: The power of prayer and the practice of medicine. New York: Harper.

Dossey, Larry. (1997). Prayer is good medicine: How to reap the healing benefits of prayer. New York: First Harper Collins.

Dyer, Kirsti. (2002). Psychoneuroimmunology. Retrieved April 30, 2004, from http://www.journeyofhearts.org/jofh/transition/pni_art.

Friedman, H., Klein, T.W., & Friedman, A.L. (1996). Psychoneuroimmunology, stress and infection. Boca Raton, FL: CRC Press.

Fritz, H. L., & Hegelson, V. S. (1998). Distinctions of unmitigated communion from communion: Self-neglect and over-involvement with others. Journal of Personality and Social Psychology, 75, 121-140.

Gerber, Richard. (2000). A practical guide to vibrational medicine: Energy healing and spiritual transformation. New York: HarperCollins.

Glaser, R., & Kiecolt-Glaser, J. K. (2005). Stress-induced immune dysfunction: Implications for health. Nature Reviews: Immunology, 5(3), 243-251.

Goodwin, Brian. (2005, August 3). Patterns of wholeness [Electronic Version]. Resurgence, 216.

Gordon, A., Merenstein, J. H., D'Amico, F., & Hudgens, D. (1998). The effects of therapeutic touch on patients with osteoarthritis of the knee. Journal of Family Practice, 47(4), 271-277.

Gruber, B. L., Hersh, S. P., Hall, N. R., Waletzky, L. R., Kunz, J. F., Carpenter, J. K., et al. (1993). Immunological responses of breast cancer patients to behavioral interventions. Biofeedback and self-regulation, 18(21), 1-22.

Hay, Louise L. (1984). You can heal your life. Carlsbad, CA: Hay House.

Hallberg, L. R., & Carlsson, S. G. (1998). Psychosocial vulnerability and maintaining forces related to fibromyalgia: In-depth interviews with twenty-two female patients. Scandinavian Journal of Caring Sciences, 12(2), 95-103.

Hillman, James (1996). The soul's code (cassette recording). New York: Random House.

Jamison, J. R. (1999). A psychological profile of fibromyalgia patients: A chiropractic case study. Journal of manipulative and physiological therapeutics, 22(7), 454-457.

Judith, Anodea. (1996). Eastern body, Western mind. Berkeley: Celestial Arts.

Justice, Blair. (2000). Who gets sick: How beliefs, moods, and thoughts affect your health. Houston: Peak Press.

Kiecolt-Glaser, J. K., & Glaser, R. (2002). Depression and immune function: Central pathways to morbidity and mortality. Journal of Psychosomatic Research, 53(4), 873-876.

Kiecolt-Glaser, J. K., Kennedy, S., Malkoff, S., Fisher, L., Speicher, C. E., & Glaser, R. (1988) Marital discord and immunity in males. Psychosomatic Medicine, 50(3), 213-219.

Larson, Daniel. (2003). Spirituality's potential relevance to physical and emotional health: A brief review of quantitative research. Journal of Psychology and Theology, 31(1), 37-51.

Lewis, Nola. (1994). Belief and survival. Noetic Sciences Review, 29, 39.

Martin-Neville, Dorothy. (2002). Dreams are only the beginning: Becoming who you were meant to be. New York: The Floating Gallery

Martin-Neville, Dorothy. (2002). Dreams are only the beginning: Companion workbook. New York: The Floating Gallery.

Myss, Caroline. (1996). Anatomy of the spirit. New York: Three Rivers Press.

Newton, Michael. (1994). Journey of souls. St. Paul: Llewellyn.

Pearsall, Paul. (1998). The heart's code. New York: Broadway Books.

Pierrakos, John. (1990). Core energetics: Developing the capacity to love and heal. CA: Liferhythms.

Pert, Candace. (1997). Molecules of emotion: The science behind mind-body medicine. New York: Touchstone.

Pignatelli, D., Magalhaes, M. C., & Magalhaes, M. M. (1998). Direct effects of stress on adrenocortical function. Hormone and Metabolism Research, 30(6-7), 464-474.

Robins, Shani, & Novaco, Raymond. (2000). Anger control as a health promotion mechanism. In David I. Mostofsky, & David H. Barlow (Eds.) The management of stress and anxiety in medical disorders (pp.361-377). Boston: Allyn & Bacon.

Siegel, Bernie. (1986). Love, medicine and miracles. New York: Harper and Row.

Shapiro, Deb. (2006). Your body speaks your mind. Boulder: Sounds True.

Spiegel, D. (1997). Healing words, emotional expression and disease outcome. Journal of the American Medical Association, 281(14), 1328-1329.

Starkweather, A., Witek-Janusek, L., & Mathews, H. L. (2005). Applying the psychoneuroimmunology framework to nursing research. Journal of Neuroscience Nursing, 37(1), 56-62.

Suhr, Julia. (2003). Neuropsychological impairment in fibromyalgia relationship to depression, fatigue, and pain. Journal of Psychosomatic Research, 55, 321-329.

Sullivan, M.J., & Bishop, S.R. (1995). The pain catastrophizing scale: Development and validation. Psychological Assessments, 7, 524-532.

Sylvia, C, & Novak, W. (1997). A change of heart: A memoir. New York: Warner Books.

Teeguarden, I. (1987). The joy of feeling: Bodymind acupressure: Jin shin do. New York: Japan Publications.

Thesenga, Susan. (2001). The undefended self. New York: Pathwork Press.

Tolle, Eckhart. (1999). The Power of now: A guide to spiritual enlightenment. CA: New World Library.

Udermann, Brian. (2000). The effect of spirituality on health and healing: A critical review for athletic trainers. Journal of Athletic Training, 35(2), 194.

Van Houdenhove, B., Vasquez, G., & Neerinckn, E. (1994). Tender points or tender patients? The value of the psychiatric in-depth interview for assessing and understanding psychopathological aspects of fibromyalgia. Clinical Rheumatology, 13(3), 470-474.

Waylonis, G.W., Ronan, P. G., & Gordon, C. (1994). A profile of fibromyalgia in occupational environments. American Journal of Physical Medicine and Rehabilitation, 73, 112-115.

Weiss, Brian. (1988). Many lives, many masters: The true story of a prominent psychiatrist, his young patient and the past life therapy that changes both their lives. New York: Simon & Schuster.

Weiss, Brian. (1997). Only love is real: A story of soul mates reunited. New York: Warner.

Wentz, K. A., Lindberg, C., & Hallberg, L. R. (2004). Psychological functioning in women with fibromyalgia: A grounded theory study. Health Care for Women International, 25(8), 702-729.

Wilber, Ken. (2005). Foreword. In M. Schlitz, Tina Amorok, & Mark Micozzi (Eds.), Consciousness & healing: Integral approaches to mind-body medicine (xv-xxxv). St. Louis, Missouri: Elsevier Churchill Livingstone.

Wolfe, F., Smythe, H., Yunus, J., et al. (1990). The American college of rheumatology 1990 criteria for the classification of fibromyalgia. Arthritis and Rheumatism, 33, 160-172.

Yount, Garret, Yifang, Quian, & Zhang, Honglin. (2005). Changing perspectives on healing energy in traditional Chinese medicine. In M. Schlitz, Tina Amorok, & Mark Micozzi (Eds.), Consciousness & healing: Integral approaches to mind-body medicine (pp. 421-433). St. Louis: Elsevier Churchill Living.

ABOUT THE AUTHOR

Dr. Dorothy Martin-Neville has had a spiritually-based private practice in psychotherapy for over twenty five years. During that time, she increased her knowledge and enhanced her practice of treating the whole person by becoming certified in Advanced Acupressure, Reflexology, Iridology, Hypnotherapy, Jin Shin Do, Energy Medicine, and Reiki II, and studying Consegrity Therapy. She has also earned her Diplomate in Comprehensive Energy Psychology and is a Clinical Instructor at the University of Connecticut Medical School.

In 1992, she founded a private occupational school, The Institute of Healing Arts and Sciences, which offered two- and four-year Energy Medicine programs that are approved by the Connecticut Commissioner of Higher Education.

Dr. Martin-Neville created her own method of treatment, The W.I.S.E.™ Method (Wholistic, Integrated, Spiritual, Energy), and was awarded grant funding from the National Institutes of Health to research this treatment modality in working with Fibromyalgia patients.

She has also been the Co-Chair of the Advisory Board of the Frontier Medicine Grant, a two-million dollar grant given to the University of Connecticut Medical School by the NIH to research Energy Medicine. In addition, the grant supported research in cellular regeneration, and cellular reconstruction, as well as cervical and breast cancers. Her doctoral dissertation, *The Psycho/Spiritual Correlates of Physical Disorders: a New Approach to Mind/Body Research,* included both qualitative and quantitative research.

As a result of her work, The Institute of Healing Arts and Sciences had contracts for placing its interns practicing Energy Medicine as members of medical teams in more than 45 hospitals and clinics nationwide. Students were able to support patients using The W.I.S.E.™ Method in medical disciplines such as Oncology, Family Medicine, Alzheimer's units, Women's Health and Maternity, In-Patient Psychiatric units, as well as Medical and Surgical Inpatient units.

She is an inspiring and entertaining speaker, author of three books, and much sought after television and radio guest as an expert in Energy Medicine and Self-Discovery in the U.S. and abroad.

Dr. Dorothy Martin-Neville can be reached at:
dorothymartin-neville.llc@comcast.net
drdorothyct.com
860-461-7569
860-543-5629

May our

souls sing and our bodies dance,

reminding us of who we truly are.